HIDING PLACES

A Crystal Springs Romance

By

Ellen Parker

Copyright 2014 by Ellen Parker
Cover art by pro_ebookcovers
Distributed by Kindle Direct Publishing

This is a work of fiction. Names, characters, corporations, institutions, organizations, events, or locales in this novel are either the product of the author's imagination or, if real, used fictitiously. The resemblance of any character to actual persons (living or dead) is entirely coincidental.

All rights reserved. No part of this book may be reproduced in any form or by any electronic or mechanical means including information storage and retrieval systems – except in the case of brief quotations embodied in critical articles and reviews – without permission.

Dedication:

To Rance and Roy
Brothers who have been teachers, protectors, and friends to this "little sister."

Chapter One

"He's coming after you, sis."

Mona Smith tensed and straightened her spine to parallel the gray metal chair. Matt's voice grated harsh on her ears as he slowed his words through a split lip. Who beat you? She focused on her brother's face, remembering him without a black eye and dark bruises against prison orange clothing.

The clink of metal against metal caused her to glance around the plain gray room. Three other tables of inmates, confined with shackles, and their visitors talked under the watchful gaze of a uniformed Minnesota Department of Corrections officer near the door. She made a quick comparison to last week's visit at the county jail and didn't like the difference. She breathed in a little courage. If Matt could live here for two years, she would visit. After all, she was the dependable child, the big sister attempting to keep little brother out of trouble.

"Who?" She rested her palms on the table, careful not to touch her brother.

"Basil. My boss. You've met him."

She nodded as a cold shiver crossed her shoulders. Basil Berg embodied pure trouble. Matt had pointed him out months ago with a warning not to get involved. From what Mona picked up from stray bits of conversation, Basil's primary revenue source was party drugs. Prostitution and burglary rounded out his business. "He came into the diner twice last week."

"Not good, sis."

2

"He behaves as a customer. No reason to refuse service." He also drank iced tea with a full breakfast at three in the morning and stared at her past polite intervals. She felt like a mouse dropped into a snake's cage when he looked her direction. "Why is he coming after me?"

Matt glanced toward the guard before dropping his voice even lower. "Money. Twenty-five grand."

"That's a year's wages. I don't have that sort of cash." Cool moisture gathered on Mona's neck. She separated her hands to reach for a tissue before realizing her pockets were empty. The only possession the officials let her bring into this room was a bright orange key to the locker in the reception area. "If I did—"

"I know." Matt lifted one slight shoulder. "You'd pay off Mother's final medical bills."

"It's the honest thing to do." She sealed her lips before the beginning of their late mother's basic monologue on the advantage of truth over expediency slipped out. She'd be visiting her brother at a Minneapolis park or coffee shop instead of prison if he'd taken that advice. "How did Basil get the notion I have money?"

Matt rubbed the three stars tattooed on his right forearm. "He got bad information. One of his minions convinced him I withheld a portion of his take on the pawnshop heist. I didn't. Always gave him his cut on assignments."

"Then—"

"I freelanced. A few jobs. Small stuff. Neighbor of the old lady they accuse me of assaulting. One or two profitable break-ins the week before. You don't need the details." Matt dipped his face to rub one ear with a manacled hand. "Didn't get near the amount his imaginative lackey reported. But Basil's prone to believe what he wants."

"He gives me the creeps." And watches me like a predator. "Should I call the police if I see that flashy ride of his near the apartment?"

"No." Matt jerked back, his chains clattering against the metal table, and the guard gave them a hard look. He eased forward again and lowered his voice to soft conversation volume. "Don't call the cops on Basil—ever. And for your information, he drives a restored El Camino."

She studied his face, and rated the expression as panic level twelve on a scale of ten. "Why shouldn't I call the cops on him?"

"You'd have another funeral to arrange. I didn't walk into a door." He pointed first to his face and then to several bruises along the edge of his prison clothes. "Initiation. All I did was walk across the yard. Basil's inside men play rough."

"I'm leaving the apartment in two weeks." She paused for an instant. Would his next sentence change her plans again? Her friend offered cheap rent but she didn't want to put another person in danger. "I'm moving in—"

"Don't tell me." A shake of his head reinforced his words. "Don't tell anyone. Just do it."

"It's that bad?" Mona rubbed her thumbs in lieu of asking the questions popping up like poisonous mushrooms after a rain. How much was Basil capable of? Could he order a murder to occur inside prison? Like a movie? She refused to put Matt's life at further risk. The two of them only had each other. She chose not to count Aunt Lucy in Duluth. Mother's sister was nice, she'd even helped with the funeral expenses, but their bond with her didn't run deep.

"You know what to do."

She nodded. Through the years they'd discussed several ways Matt could leave the Twin Cities and start fresh. Half of them involved a vanishing act before looking up their father. It'd been three years since the last letter from Joseph Ignatius Smith. She closed her eyes and thought hard for a moment, but the name of the city in Washington State on the envelope didn't come. In all their bantered planning through the years she'd never thought she'd be the one needing to run. "I don't want to abandon you."

"I'm past your help. You need to take care of you." He leaned forward to the invisible midline of the table.

She sighed. Matt was right. She needed to get away, give Basil and his drug organization time to forget her. I'll start when I get home. A list of actions to take, beginning with giving notice and asking for a reference at the diner, had already started in the list-making portion of her mind. She'd find a place to land and seek work. She could waitress. Or cook. Or work as a maid.

"Two minutes, visitors." The guard announced the imminent end of their time together.

"Until next time?" Matt looked up from his handcuffs and stared into her eyes.

"Yes. Next time." She struggled with the lump in her throat representing how long to "next time." Would it be weeks? Months? When she walked out of this windowless room and back into an early June afternoon, would it be up to Matt to find her after his two-year sentence? She stared into his deep, dark eyes and memorized the face too worn for twenty-three years. "Take care, little brother."

* * *

Mona opened the brass mailbox and tucked the contents into her waistband. A moment later she unlocked the apartment building's interior door and headed for the stairs. Bits and pieces of Matt's conversation continued to chase each other, undeterred by the three bus transfers, two-block walk, and pleasant spring weather.

Will I visit the prison again? She grasped the wooden handrail at the memory of all the negative aspects of the visit. Even after researching the facility, the sheer size had nearly overwhelmed her. She'd expected rules and formality, but not the extent of the difference with the county jail.

He's coming after you. Initiation. Matt's words, plus the tone of voice used to say them, were enough to keep a person awake at night. Her self-assigned duty to protect Matt needed to be put on hold. He told her to take care of herself. The best way to be the good big sister in this case was to get away from Basil's reach.

She paused, adjusted a backpack strap, and listened to the soft thud of the elevator doors half a flight above her. The elderly motor started, hesitated, and began again with a steady growl. Even after three years in this building the sound still brought thoughts of a tiger staking claim to supper. She continued her climb to the third floor.

6

A few moments later Mona tensed in front of her apartment. The door, so carefully closed and locked behind her this morning, showed a sliver of air between the frame and panel. She threaded her keys between the fingers of her right hand and nudged the door open with her foot.

Silence. And—smoke? A cigar? She eased inside and stifled a gasp. Drawers and their contents lay scattered across the living room floor. The closet door stood open, the boxes from the shelf strewn on the carpet. To her left, the Murphy bed doors were flung wide, the bed pulled a third of the way down like a monster emerging from the wall.

He's coming after you. For an instant the room sucked her into a gray whirlpool. She sagged, rested one shoulder against the wall, and wrapped her arms in a self-hug. Basil carried cigars. He'd been here—moments ago. Had she avoided him only by taking the stairs? She concentrated on taking her next breath.

The plans for her disappearance tomorrow, plotted during the long bus ride, vanished. She needed to go. Now. Forget giving notice at work. Jennifer, her best friend, would have to cope without a phone call.

Mona hurried to the bedroom and began to fill her backpack. She picked up enough clean clothes from the confusion in front of the dresser to last a few days. Documents and papers from one of the drawers lay across the bed and she gathered two large handfuls, stuffed them under her best jeans in the backpack, and added today's mail to the stash. In the bathroom she grabbed only her toothbrush and small cosmetic case. Money. She carried seventeen dollars and a transit card in her pockets. Not enough.

She took her full pack across the defiled living room and dropped it beside a tipped dinette chair. Both hands swept up to block her mouth as her foot touched the kitchen vinyl. *I will not scream.* She forced her gaze to move across the kitchen from top to bottom, left to right. Every cabinet door hung open. Flatware, broken china, and kitchen gadgets lay on every flat surface. A tipped bottle of olive oil dripped into a mound of rice on the floor.

One step forward, then another, she forced her body to move until she stood by the sink. In the photo, she stood, smiling, at the diner's cashier station. Now the picture was fastened to a thick cutting board with her best boning knife, the tip through the base of her throat. Red marker repeated the threat: "I'm coming."

She reached back, pulled out her phone, and flipped it open. Her fingers dialed without an order from her brain.

"Emergency services. May I help you?"

"Uh." She gripped the phone and sealed her lips. *Matt. Never call the police on Basil.* She couldn't put his life at greater risk. He was all her family that mattered. "No. I'm sorry. It's been a mistake."

She snapped the phone shut and tossed it into the trash.

Within two minutes she'd retrieved the cloth bag of cash from the never-used electric teakettle. By rare good luck it had escaped notice in the back of a base cabinet. On her way to the door she added her Chinese grandparents' wedding photo, cracked glass and all, plus the framed portrait of her mother, to her luggage. She settled the backpack on her shoulders before snatching a pastel blue ball cap and her windbreaker from the closet floor. In the doorway she turned for a final look and blew a kiss to the apartment of memories.

"Fastest way out of town." She muttered her need as she hurried down three flights of stairs. She discarded the idea of the bus; during the wait at the Greyhound station she'd be a target. She needed something quick and private. She exited the apartment building and turned away from her usual bus stop. Six blocks away she could catch a train at the light rail platform. From there—

She crossed the first side street, and hurried her steps. At the next cross street she tensed at a glimpse of bright red paint and polished chrome. She blinked, confirmed it was Basil's restored classic El Camino, and pulled in a deep breath.

Walk. Don't run or act guilty. Mona crushed her windbreaker against her chest and marched toward the light rail stop.

Chapter Two

Linc Dray ignored the airport overhead speakers and merged onto the escalator. How many times had he listened to the unattended baggage script today? He could probably recite it backward if given a minute or two. The only difference appeared to be the name of the airport. The air filled with a recorded voice again, this time starting, "Welcome to Minneapolis/St. Paul International." He walked in the herd from his flight toward a digital sign over the baggage carousal.

Wanted: single female, age 21-30. He reviewed the first line of the ad overdue to be posted on the regional Craigslist. Desire quick marriage? Seeking long-term relationship? No, he discarded the second line as tacky. The truth in the mental discard file mattered less as the days counted down. Today left thirteen. Less than two weeks to find a woman, convince her he wasn't a pervert or serial killer, and legally marry.

If he failed, his grandfather's farm would be sold to strangers. Last year, when he'd discovered his grandparents wrote the will so that he could only inherit if married within a year of his grandmother's death, he hadn't panicked. He and Tami were a steady couple. She accepted his ring a month later and set a date.

And blindsided me three weeks before the wedding. He reached up and rubbed at the tension in his neck. In one winter afternoon she'd deflated years of hopes. He could see his dream, expanding the tiny orchard to a viable business, blowing away quicker than apple blossoms on a sudden gust of wind. Most likely, go corporate. He shook his head at the idea that a farm passed down through a family for more than a century would become no more than a line entry on a spreadsheet.

Twice he scrolled through his mental list of single former classmates and co-workers. Each of them ranked less promising than the sister of a friend he'd just visited. There was not one hint of hesitation or uncertainty in her negative answer yesterday. Until she'd realized the arrangement included a move to rural Wisconsin, she'd been open to the idea of a quick marriage. But she had the beginning of a good career in Texas and intended to stay.

Another announcement broke his silent review. He stepped forward and a moment later spotted luggage from the Dallas flight sliding onto the conveyer. He adjusted the computer bag slung over his shoulder and snatched the suitcase with stickers of President Lincoln's profile plastered next to the handles.

"You're here." A young woman called out the words an instant before her head collided with his chest. Her arms wrapped around his waist, pulling them together.

Linc's body automatically began a retreat, and managed half a step with her following every inch. He tipped his face down and discovered smooth, youthful features half concealed by a blue cap decorated with the Pillsbury Dough Boy. Pickpocket?

"Help me. Act like we're friends." She clung tight and dropped her voice to keep the words private.

"Because?" He glanced around, not sure what he was looking for. His fellow passengers from the flight ignored them in favor of their own baggage and family reunions. A trio of business travelers walked past.

"There's a man, black T-shirt and tattooed arms, following me. He's a criminal." She eased away half a step without breaking the circle around him.

Linc reached back and separated her hands, retained a grip on one, and brought it forward. Her dainty fingers clung to him, sending a dual message of desperation and warmth into his arm. "There's uniformed security by door number three."

"It's complicated."

He laughed one syllable. "Story of my life."

"Please. I won't be trouble."

He looked over his shoulder and spotted a man fitting her hurried description. Did she tell the truth? Or was the muscular man on the phone her partner in an illegal scheme? He tightened his grip on her with one hand and jerked out his suitcase handle with the other before taking one long step. "Let's walk. Who are you?"

"Call me ..." She swallowed. "Mona."

Hesitation on a simple question. Linc angled their path and glanced first at her and then the man. His experience with women uncertain of their own name hadn't existed until a moment ago. Then again, the man she'd indicated did have an unsettling air about him.

"My name's Linc. That's short for Lincoln Dray. The man following you, is he holding a phone and walking out of door number two?"

"Yes, that's him."

"Looks dangerous."

"He is."

He halted in front of a lighted board advertising local attractions before dropping her hand. Tiny. Young. He touched his back pocket and confirmed she hadn't lifted his wallet. "I could be just as hazardous. What do you need?"

She fingered both straps of her bulging backpack and looked him full in the face. "I need to get out of the city. Give time for his temper to cool or get distracted."

He scanned the people around him and let the questions in his mind jostle for priority. "Why me? I could live a mile away."

"With that hat?" She sent a cautious smile toward him.

He adjusted the brim of his Milwaukee Brewers baseball cap and nodded. "Mona, how old are you?"

She raised both black straight brows, giving him a better look at the darkest, most alluring set of eyes he'd ever seen.

"Twenty-four."

"You look closer to fifteen." His gaze fastened on her face, looking for clues beyond smooth cheeks and a small mouth presenting a large dose of determination. "I'm not eager to get arrested as soon as I cross a state line."

"Do I need to prove it?"

"Yes."

"Will you return the favor?"

He looked over his shoulder to confirm the man she feared was out of sight before pulling out his wallet and flipping it open to his Wisconsin driver's license.

A moment later she extended a Minnesota identification card into his view.

"Smith, Mary Monica? I expected something more exotic." He held his mouth neutral as he calculated her age to match her previous answer. Officially she claimed to be an even five feet tall. He inspected her again and figured that could be an exaggeration.

"I prefer Mona." She returned her ID card to her pocket. "Some of my grandparents were Chinese. I inherited my grandmother's eyes."

He reached out and snatched her cap. A mound of straight black hair fell past her chin.

"Hey. Give me my hat." She rose up on her toes and reached high, unable to win against his additional height and longer arm.

"Maybe later. I can see you better without it." He looked directly into her unique eyes and fought the pull of twin whirlpools tugging him to the depths. "By the way, your non-friend left."

"I need. I want." She stepped closer and brushed against him while attempting to claim her cap.

"It's not much of a disguise."

"I was in a hurry. Will you give me a ride? Drop me off at a motel near that Eau Claire address on your ID?"

"I'll think about it." He inspected her, and cataloged a serious, determined expression out of place on her youthful face. Would she do? Did a gift in answer to that stream of prayers he'd sent in recent months stand in front of him? Or did she represent a cruel joke of the fates sent to lull him into a trap?

He crossed pickpocket off his list of her possible occupations as he returned his wallet to its usual place and pulled his keys into one palm.

Gooseflesh rippled along his arms at the thought she could have picked a different stranger, one who would have no moral or ethical problem taking advantage of her situation. He studied her for another long moment, telling himself that small and weak were very different things. Her backpack appeared full and heavy, yet she carried it with ease. Her posture, arms, and what he could tell of her legs in black pants indicated an athlete. He'd play it cautious and treat her as capable of putting a man into a painful position with one quick jab in a vital place.

"My next stop is an Econoline van in the blue parking ramp. If you follow I'll give you a ride out of the city. Fair enough?"

* * *

Mona snatched her cap out of Linc's fingers while his arm was still in motion. She gathered her hair into a messy twist and settled the hat over it. It wasn't good, not even as neat as her previous quick attempt on the train, but it would conceal her black hair from a casual observer. She glanced back to the small group still at the baggage carousel and breathed relief. The man in the clerical collar, whom she'd almost selected over the Brewers cap, hugged a woman. Must be one of those Protestant look-alikes.

The automatic door opened with a swish and she hurried to catch up with Linc. One final hesitation attacked as she walked past the security guard and he made eye contact. One shout, three steps, and she could report Basil's suspicious behavior. Nope. Not worth it. The apartment might have enough evidence to tie Basil to the break-in. But he'd have a rational story to explain following her on the train to the airport.

Matt had warned her to stay away from the police. She'd almost tripped up at the apartment with the aborted phone call. It had been difficult enough to look at his bruises; she wasn't going to risk his life. No police. She would remember Matt's simple request. It blended into her own wariness of law enforcement developed during her brother's descent into criminal activity. In her experience they arrested first and brushed off explanations far too easily.

Basil took this exit. She kept her gaze in motion, imagining the gang leader watching from behind a pillar or shadowed alcove. Was he alone? Or did he have one or more of his minions tailing her?

She held her breath as Linc led them into an elevator and pressed the button for one of the lower levels. What if? What if this stranger she'd selected on the basis of clean-cut appearance and out-of-town baseball cap had evil intent? Did they have security cameras in here?

"Row D, five or six spaces from the far end." Linc glanced back as he exited the tiny, isolated elevator.

"Okay." She needed to take three steps for every two of his long strides. Stale auto exhaust mingled in early summer humidity and wrapped around concrete pillars decorated with white letters on blue squares.

He's given me time and opportunity to leave. Does that confirm his honesty? Or conceal a practiced liar?

She glanced at his profile when they paused for a car. How tall had his license listed him? She'd been more interested in the address. He might be an inch under six feet. He impressed her as long arms and legs on a lean, fit torso. His ringless fingers wrapped around the suitcase handle. She met pale grey eyes for an instant before returning her gaze to the stairway beside the elevator.

A shadow moved up the steps and her heart did a little hesitation thing, imitating the uncertain moment of water between simmer and boil. She blinked, stepped off behind Linc with her attention on the stairwell and glimpsed an arm. Is that tattooed?

"What sort of car are we looking for?" She kept her voice steady while sensing a flash behind them. Another. Like a photographer ensuring his shot.

"White van. Ford. Commercial configuration." He led her across an aisle, his words attempting to echo on the harsh walls.

Her legs steadied with confidence. No matter what the man beside her turned out to be, she'd found a breathing spell. A ride out of the city remained all she wanted. All Lincoln Dray volunteered.

One more obstacle now delayed Basil, or whoever he'd sent after her, before they could try to take money she didn't have. She said a quick prayer for Matt, that her escape from the dark world represented by Basil wouldn't bring retaliation. Matt regretted his slide into the illegal lifestyle. He'd made that clear over and over by keeping her away from his friends and the criminal culture's black grasp as best he could.

* * *

"Be here in ten." Basil Berg snapped the words into his smartphone. He pictured Nick, his subordinate at the other end of the command, sprinting to his car. In the interim Basil needed to collect more information. He hurried back into the stairwell and down one level.

The Smith girl and her new friend walked along the aisle in the parking ramp, ready to get ahead of him. According to the plate on the white van, the driver lived in Wisconsin. He dared to hope she stayed with him instead of pulling a fancy multi-layered exit from the metro area.

He paused on the final landing above Matt's sister and confirmed he was alone on this portion of the stairwell. He eased forward and spotted the white Econoline backing into the aisle.

Click. Click. Click. He added three images with the maximum telephoto setting on his phone before stepping back into the shadows. Never hurt to have another view.

Basil thought about Mona's greeting to the young man. The van driver had arrived on the American flight from Dallas. Did she know him? Or was she an actress? He'd bet a baggie of his best Molly on the latter. Matt didn't claim a lot of relatives. That gave the girl the same low number. If this man belonged to the Caucasian side of the family he'd have been at the mother's funeral. Basil reflected again on that late January day and didn't recall any mourner who came close to tall, blond, and young. Nope. All he could picture at the moment were a collection of hotel employees, including men of an older generation, and ladies from the Chinese community.

If this was a new close friend, he'd missed any mention of it during visits to the diner. He'd approach the situation as Mona trusting a random stranger. Not the sort of behavior he expected from her.

Basil descended one more step to get a clearer view as the van circled toward the exit. He snapped three front-view photos before footsteps prompted him to continue down the stairs. He walked to the elevator, waited for a family to count children and luggage, and pushed the button for the main pick-up level.

Five minutes later, Basil slipped into the passenger side of a Ford Escape and clicked the seat belt almost before the vehicle came to a rest.

"Where to, boss?" Nick eased back into the traffic of the Terminal One passenger pick-up lane.

"Franklin. Five hundred block. I need to pick up my car."

"Why didn't you drive here?"

"Wrong question." The girl had taken the train and he'd followed, but Nick didn't have the need to know. Basil met Nick's quick glance with a stare to confirm the chain of command. He would not have any employee, even a capable man like Nick, prying into his private business. At this moment his driver needed an address, nothing more.

Basil did a quick mental review of his search in the Smith apartment. Not one piece of jewelry or trendy small electronics—which Matt favored in his burglaries—turned up. The situation looked more and more like his informant had passed along a personal gripe against Matt. Still, Basil needed to confront the girl, get a second opinion of Matt's activities when not on assignments. Besides, she was a pretty little thing, hard-working at the diner. She appeared to be the sort of person a man could take home to his mother.

"Can you work with the photos?" Basil made a follow-up call to his personal contact at motor vehicles.

"Wisconsin plates. Green bumper sticker's consistent with a school ... cougar mascot. It's going to take time. I'm not at the office and will need to hack into the official database."

"It's top priority." He needed to get a tail on the girl. Tomorrow, after this other situation settled, he'd pay her a personal visit.

Basil disconnected the call and maintained silence until Nick scooted into a parking place half a block from Mona's apartment.

"Ten o'clock tonight. Bring a name to go with that rogue dealer," Basil instructed Nick as he exited the car. He wanted to have his facts straight before he acted against a punk selling his exclusive brand, the double B butterfly logo, on ecstasy.

"Right, boss." For an instant Nick appeared ready to speak again but showed the good sense to hold it back.

"Now, go." Basil slapped the roof of the car once before walking forward to give a quick inspection to his waiting vehicle. Satisfied that the chrome and tires remained in pristine condition, he leaned against the passenger door of his 1967 metallic red El Camino and dialed the second largest hospital in the city.

"This is Basil Berg. Tell me if Kevin Berg has been admitted. He'll be coming in from Twin Pines Residential Facility."

"What is your relationship, sir?" A tired feminine voice came over a background of assorted chimes and distant conversation.

"Brother. You should have my name on all his paperwork. He's been a patient with you before." He swallowed back an epithet the receptionist didn't deserve for following a script. By now he could probably recite the confidentiality rules in his sleep.

"Sir?"

"Yes, I'm still on the line."

"We show him as registered in orthopedic emergency."

Basil thanked the woman and tapped his phone to a calendar application. Sure enough, Kevin's seizures were getting more frequent. Only three days since the previous episode. According to the staff at Kevin's home, this one had come on so suddenly and severely they suspected a broken ankle from thrashing against furniture. He'd have to discuss that most recent medication change with the doctor in charge.

Three years ago Kevin Berg had been a college sophomore with a bright future. But an accident on an icy road resulted in a traumatic brain injury. Now he struggled to dress and eat without assistance.

Basil pulled out of the parking space and drove at the exact speed limit toward the hospital. Matt Smith, his sister, and the missing money slipped down in priority. His brother needed him.

Chapter Three

Mona twisted in the confines of her seat belt and scanned the rear interior of the van. A large rubber mat covered the central portion of a metal floor. A set of shelves appeared bolted along the driver's side almost to the rear door. She didn't see dirt, but she could smell it, almost feel it in her hand. "Smells like a greenhouse."

"I expect it does." Linc pulled away from the parking ramp payment booth.

"Is that where you work?" The realization she knew nothing about the man beside her collided with years of warnings from family and teachers like an invisible punch to her stomach.

He fished a business card out of the cup holder in the console between them and held it out. "I do interior gardens."

She took her gaze off the maze of traffic signs and read the green script next to a design of ivy overflowing from a pot. "Terrier's Plant Services. It doesn't match your name."

"I'm not the owner."

She held her breath as he sped up while merging into traffic on a different interstate. City streets suited her better. She felt comfortable riding her bicycle between work, school, the apartment, and several Minneapolis parks. When she took the bus on longer jaunts she kept track of landmarks and key streets. This maze with overhead green signs and arrows giving the choice of three directions confused her.

"Are you okay over there? Having second thoughts?"

Third and fourth. She forced an exhale. "I'll be okay. Not used to the traffic."

"It's the beginning of the evening rush. Pardon me while I concentrate on driving for a bit. I'll drop you off in a few miles if you want. Just speak up and I'll exit before it gets rural."

"No." She put a fake firmness in her reply. "Take me to Eau Claire. Drop me off at a modest motel."

"Yes, ma'am." He checked his mirrors and eased into a different lane.

Mona rested her feet on her bulging backpack and tucked the business card into her pocket, next to her transit Go-To Card. The opportunity for a garden, interior or exterior, lay outside the confines of her life. Maybe, after they got away from the worst of this traffic, she'd prod him for specifics.

"Who is he?" Linc shot a glance in her direction after a few moments of silence.

"What do you mean?"

"Are you running from your husband?"

She burst into a short laugh. "I've never been married. And certainly not to him."

"A boyfriend? An ex?"

"No. And no again. He …" She touched her lips with two fingers to bundle her thoughts differently. "My brother worked for him. He belongs in prison, but he manages to be smoother than a nonstick pan when arrested."

"And your brother? What sort of coating does he have?"

She turned her head to watch his reaction. It might just be necessary to take an exit before the state line after all. "Velcro."

He looked away and checked the mirrors as if buying time before a reply.

"Before you ask, I don't work with my brother. He's a thief currently serving time for breaking and entering." She stopped before adding the assault charge, the item on the list that put him in state prison instead of county jail. The one crime he'd tried and failed to get the public defender to fight. In the end he'd taken a plea for a minimum sentence. She knew he was innocent. Wrong time, wrong place, with jewelry from the neighbors on his person.

"Then why not talk to the security guard? Or the police?" He sped past the final Minnesota exit.

"It gets complicated."

"We've got almost seventy miles of highway to discuss it."

"We're strangers."

"New acquaintances."

Mona settled back into her seat and considered his word choice. Did she want to become acquainted? It would be safer to keep the conversation general. Her exit plan from Minneapolis changed so fast it blurred. Get to Eau Claire. Walk away clean from Mr. Lincoln Dray. Find a cheap, safe place to spend the night. Then—big question without answers. "Sometimes I talk too much."

"I've been guilty of the opposite." He settled the van behind an eighteen-wheeler and gestured toward her footrest. "Tell me about Mona Smith and her college backpack."

"Culinary student." The words popped out before her brain could arrange an evasive response. "I'm trying for duel certificates in culinary and restaurant management. But school's been put on indefinite hold."

"While you run away from criminals?"

"My studies were interrupted before today." She looked out the window but instead of seeing young corn and soybean plants in neat rows, she remembered her final real conversation with her mother.

"Only one class this term?" Mona's mother asked over a lap filled with another afghan in progress.

"It's all I can afford. Tips have been down. Don't worry, it's required for the management certificate and meets five days a week. I'll be busy enough."

"Maybe you'll meet a nice young man this time." Her mother smiled and continued with the crochet hook.

"Dating takes time away from other things. Anyway, I've not met any interesting young men for over a year now. Aren't you the one always telling me to be patient?"

"My hopes for you include a family. Is that so bad?"

"Not at all. I'm just not in a hurry."

The very next day her mother collapsed at work. Twelve days and two surgeries later her body gave up the fight.

"What happened?"

Linc's question pulled her back to the present. "Financial problems came up."

* * *

"Ever hear of a town named Crystal Springs?" Linc interrupted one of their frequent calm silences. Each of their tiny conversations so far supplied another tidbit or two of intriguing information. In his imagination he viewed his knowledge of Mona growing from a sprouting seed to a tender plant putting out the first and then second set of leaves.

Nothing contradicted the idea growing in his mind. This evening he'd get on the computer and take Daryl up on the offer of a free background check. He already knew enough basics to get the investigator pointed in the right direction. Thirteen days. How big a gamble was he willing to take?

"I don't think so. How far away is it?" Mona pulled her hair into a ponytail and secured it with an elastic band she'd dug out of a pocket.

"It's near the Mississippi, in River County."

She nodded. "I've heard that name mentioned on the storm warnings."

"So you learn geography courtesy of the National Weather Service?"

"Every spring."

"Hey. Whatever works." He sorted through a dozen questions sprouting in his mind. "My roots are there."

"Do you have lots of family in ... Crystal Springs?"

"Not now. Unless cemetery plots count." Stop it. "The family still owns land. An entire farm three miles out of town, up on the hill."

"I've never visited a real farm. I think I'm a city girl from fingers to toes and all the stops between."

"Interesting description."

She shrugged. "Whatever works."

"The orchard's on that land." He glanced over and confirmed she was paying attention. "My dream is to develop a viable apple orchard on the place. I planted a thousand trees before I ran into a problem."

"Major?"

"Big as they get."

"I'm familiar with extra-large economy-sized trouble." She sighed.

"I'm thinking one of yours is named Basil." He checked the mile marker and fought the urge to slow down and extend their time together.

"Today he moved past money and brother to top of the list."

"Something will come up."

"The next exit will be fine. I'll have my choice of motels and restaurants."

"Save your money. I've got a better idea." He ignored the exit with large tourist service signs. Will you marry me?

* * *

Mona's senses went on full alert the moment Linc bypassed the exit with multiple services displayed. What had she missed? Men and their "better ideas" made a sensible girl nervous. She concentrated on memorizing every sign in sight and keeping her panic from spilling out of her skin.

Linc took the next highway exit, managed to catch a green left turn arrow at the top of the ramp, and continued too fast for more than keeping her fingers on the seat belt release. She needed the van at a complete stop for more than five seconds to get the door open, grab her pack, and scurry out.

"We're home." Linc hit the garage door opener an instant before he turned from narrow asphalt street to cement parking pad.

Time for me to go. She released her seat belt, grabbed her backpack with her left hand, and unlatched the door with her right. "Thanks for the ride. You've done more than enough."

"Hey. No need to panic." He set the transmission to "park" and reached toward her.

"You helped me. I appreciate it. I'm going now." She shouldered her pack as soon as both feet hit solid ground. So much for the fantasy twenty miles back of parting as friends. She won the battle over impulse. Brisk steps, rather than a sprint, moved her away from the place Linc called home.

He got out of the van and followed her. "Hey. Talk to me."

Wrong time and place. She aimed her steps toward the street sign at the corner.

"Let me explain. I didn't mean to scare you."

Too late. When she arrived at the sign, Benson Place, she turned to go up a small slope and risked a glance down the quiet street. A little tension shed off her body at confirmation he remained well away from her. She marked a mental point in his favor for not running in pursuit.

Mona walked three blocks to the convenience store beside a stoplight before she risked another look back. From this position she could see the turn-off to the subdivision and a row of roofs in various shades of gray. She spit out the smell of earth from his van into the grass.

Did all men lack common sense? During the drive Linc claimed to live alone—no roommate, no wife, no girlfriend. And he expected her to walk into the house beside him? Did he ever listen to the news? Did he have a clue of the fright and caution a man's strength radiated to a small woman, even a veteran of a college self-defense class?

A few minutes later she set an energy drink and granola bar on the store counter and reached for money. A few crumpled bills and Linc's business card came into view.

"Is that all?" The clerk scanned the first item.

"I have a question." She glanced around and gathered a little courage. "Do you happen to know Lincoln Dray? He lives down the hill a couple of blocks."

While the clerk took his time to reply she fought off another image prompted by the smell of dirt in the van. "Drives a white van, delivery type, not many windows," she added.

"Not on a first-name basis with many of my customers."

"He's young, maybe thirty. Six feet, blond … gray eyes. Goes by Linc."

"Beginning to sound familiar now. If it's the man I'm thinking of he stops in for milk or ice cream couple of times a week."

Relief seeped out with her next breath. Buying milk established residence in the neighborhood at the most. She gathered her change and broke the seal on her drink. "One more question." She pointed toward the sheltered bench at the edge of the property. "How often does the bus come past?"

"Once an hour at this time of day. Should be one along in ten or fifteen minutes."

"Thank you." Time to explore. She knew little about Eau Claire aside from it being home to a university and larger than the neighboring cities in western Wisconsin. She figured two hours of good daylight remained to explore and find a safe place to stay the night. And if she was lucky, she'd gather a little information on Mr. Dray.

Chapter Four

Linc threaded his way against the flow of students headed into Phillips Science Hall for Friday morning classes. Twelve days. He frowned into sunshine outside the glass walkway at the realization he needed to cut the number in half due to Wisconsin's waiting period. Yeah, his boss still offered tickets to Las Vegas, but he considered that beyond his current state of desperation. For a long moment he cataloged the students coming through the door and shook his head. Even in the summer session too many were below full legal age.

A moment later he continued into a fine, early June day. The weather promised to be hot later, but now the air bathed his skin with perfect shirtsleeve temperatures. Today was one in which to savor his outdoor moments between errands and client calls – as soon as he got a cup of Kona coffee. Odd as it may seem, the University of Wisconsin-Eau Claire served the best brew he'd found in the student center café.

Carrying a large paper cup of steaming liquid, Linc turned away from the cashier a few minutes later and surveyed the dining area. He headed for an empty table with a good view of a young crabapple tree. Halfway across the room he came to a complete stop. Is it? He blinked twice and brought the girl near the far wall into sharp focus.

She sat in profile to him, intently studying papers covering half the table, and ignoring the murmur of activity filling the room. He walked within three feet of her while silently sorting out opening lines. "Mona?"

"You." She turned her face to him, widened her dark, amazing eyes, and formed a perfect "O" with her lips. An instant later she turned over the papers as if to keep them secret.

"I listened for the doorbell all night."

"That was foolish."

"Not the word I'd use." He chose not to spoil the day, or this new, fortunate encounter by recalling the names he'd called himself during long, dark, futile hours. Instead he motioned to the other chair at her small table. "May I?"

"Are you following me?"

"I like the coffee here. My boss, Dr. Terrier, asked me to deliver some papers to a friend over in the biology department."

"That's all?"

"I owe you an apology for yesterday. I forgot ... forgot to see the situation from your perspective." He pulled out the chair and waited for her objection. When she merely gave a small nod he took a seat. He thought of the background check request he'd gone ahead and turned into Frieberg Investigations. If he'd not crossed paths with her today, would he have paid Daryl to find her tomorrow? "We should talk. I didn't intend to scare you away."

"What did you plan? I needed a little help to flee from a dangerous man. I spoke clearly and concisely when I asked to be dropped off at a public place." She toyed with the cap of a sports drink bottle. "Did I impress you as the sort of girl to walk into a worse situation?"

"I'm not dangerous. Not in the way you imply. I have an extra bedroom, complete with a lock to keep me out." He caged his hands around his cup to prevent them from touching hers. "If you're going to stay in Eau Claire you'll need a place to live. Unless that backpack of yours is filled with cash, a motel will run through your resources quick."

"I'm listening."

"Are you interested in exchanging cooking and light housekeeping for room and board?"

"You didn't think to say this before pulling into your driveway?"

"Not my finest moment." Linc concentrated on keeping his mouth neutral. He wanted to smile. A bit of him longed to explain his impulsive actions. But he recalled the flash of terror on her face when she left the van yesterday. Twelve days, less six. *She's my final chance.*

"Separate bedrooms." She put an edge of command in the words.

"Absolutely."

"I can get a day job. Or evenings, if that's what's available."

He longed to give her permission to work any hours she could find. The cooking wasn't that important. He'd offered it to salvage a fraction of the pride she displayed every time she moved her shoulders. That trace of stubborn independence attracted him as strong as a flower beckoned a bee. "I'll be flexible on the details."

She tipped her head down, as if studying the backs of the papers spread out on her side of the table.

"Do you have plans for the rest of today?" He lost the battle to avoid her and reached forward to brush his thumb across the back of her hand. The warmth of the touch startled him into a momentary retreat. Her skin felt as soft as a puppy's and twice as inviting.

She straightened, drew a deep breath, and gazed out the window. "I don't know anything about plants, if you're fishing for an assistant."

"Will you allow me to call a woman that might have a day of odd jobs for you?"

"Legal? Moral?" She raised one of her exclamation-point eyebrows.

He swallowed back a laugh and hid his lips behind the coffee cup for a moment. "My boss's wife needs to get a house ready for an estate sale. After her brother-in-law died last month, her personal life took a turn for the worse and she hasn't gotten things sorted."

"Sounds interesting."

"I'll call her." He hurried to tap a programed number before Mona could change her mind.

* * *

What have I done? Mona sealed her lips. Since he'd returned to her life by saying her name this morning, her stomach had lusted for the rich coffee aroma of his drink. And something else; a dormant kernel of curiosity planted yesterday yearned for satisfaction. It was hazy logic, or perhaps no logic at all, to agree to live with him. At his house. Separate bedrooms. Housekeeper. She closed her eyes for a moment and attempted to blame her reply on lack of sleep and caffeine.

34

While he waited for a response on his phone she began to straighten the papers she'd been studying. Yesterday's mail contained another bill from the hospital. The puzzling portion of this one was a credit of $4,812. She was grateful the bill was cut by a third but since the insurance company wasn't listed as the payer and her meager, irregular payments of a hundred dollars here and there didn't come close to this number, it was a bit of a mystery.

Who'd paid her mother's bill? Aunt Lucy? No, her mother's only sister had contributed to the funeral expenses, but she didn't have thousands to spare.

Life insurance? Nothing in Mona's correspondence with them indicated payment to the hospital. In the most recent letter they'd estimated payment in August, and for a different amount.

"Lorraine. This is Linc."

Mona shifted her attention to her table partner and his side of the conversation.

"No, I stopped for coffee at the student center." He lifted his gaze to Mona. "I may have found an assistant for your housecleaning, a young lady. I'm putting you on speaker."

"A student? Is she with you now? Available today?" A pleasant female voice drifted up from the phone laid in the center of the table.

"No. Yes. And yes." He nudged the smartphone in her direction. "Go ahead, Mona."

"Hi. Linc tells me you're getting a house ready for an estate sale." Mona skimmed her gaze up his arm, trying to catch a second glimpse of a scar. He'd turned his wrist again, shielding the interior of his forearm. Later. She sipped water from the bottle she'd refilled several times since yesterday. Lorraine asked basic questions and Mona supplied concise, truthful answers without volunteering additional information. In less than five minutes they decided that Linc would bring her to the greenhouse for a face-to-face meeting.

"See you in a few." Linc leaned into the space above the phone to finish the conversation.

Mona moistened her lips and gathered a few of her wits that had seemed to scatter each time Linc dipped past an invisible boundary to contribute to the discussion. She remained aware of her skin behaving irrationally as it begged for a repeat of his touch. Dirt from his occupation blended with shaving cream in a scent to rouse her curiosity.

"Are you good with this? Really good?" Linc reached for his coffee.

"Fine as powdered sugar." She lifted the backpack to her lap. "You have no need to look worried. Lorraine's your friend. We've talked. Unless my judge-o-meter is broken you haven't put me into the hands of a brothel madam."

He sputtered a mouthful of coffee into a napkin. "Jeeseh."

"That's a lovely shade of red you're wearing." She tempered her building laugh into a genuine smile and watched him scramble for a response.

"Sorry. I didn't see that coming. Are you sure you're not a lawyer?"

"In my experience, cops, attorneys, and drug addicts populate the lowest levels of society." She zipped the smallest pouch of her pack closed. An image of Matt's public defender intruded and she pushed against the memory of the young, inexperienced recent law school graduate. The prosecutor had presented evidence against Matt, yet Mona still wondered if a more experienced lawyer would have managed a better deal. Both she and Matt had expected probation after a few weeks in county jail—not two years in state custody.

"Ready?" Linc clipped his smartphone to his belt.

"Could I talk you into buying me one of those?" She pointed to his coffee. "I skipped caffeine this morning."

* * *

Basil jabbed the gray button to lower the metal warehouse door. Sunshine and street noise melted into low male voices and a single engine in idle. He paid close attention to timing and watched the barrier slide down mere inches behind the vehicle's tailgate and rear bumper.

He eyed the truck and driver with a mixture of suspicion and relief. His chemist was tardy, fifty minutes late without a simple status call. He rubbed his face in a futile attempt to wipe off the visible effects of too little sleep. Red Bull mixed with iced tea lacked the ability to bring him up to mental sharpness today. He broke the seal on another energy drink and observed. Patience. Confirming rumors ranks equal with capturing fog for difficulty.

"Afternoon, man." Daniel Larson jumped down from his black, double cab Dodge Ram. "Traffic's a bummer on the four thirty-five."

Basil nodded and sipped his drink while giving his chemist credit for keeping any lies plausible. He ambled toward the tall, thin man with the knowledge and facilities to manufacture the finest ecstasy and Molly available in the metro area. One more whisper. That's what I'll allow. "Do you have my order?"

"Snug as a master carpenter's joint. I created a new color for the tablets: lime green. I figured the ladies would enjoy a change." Daniel flashed a smile and extended a hand.

"Color's good. Quality's better." Basil cooperated with the briefest of handshakes. "I like my customers to be repeaters. Live addicts spend more money than one-shot over dose wonders."

"Sounds like a marketing campaign. Or a poetry attempt."

"It could be." Basil depended on word-of-mouth advertising. Twitter blasts worked to spread time and location of his raves. Constant surveillance of the initial Twitter group plus a sharp eye at the entrance continued to keep out the wrong clientele: undercover cops.

Basil beckoned two of his associates over and the four men spent the next half hour unpacking, counting, and weighing drugs. Brightly colored tablets in tiny plastic bags passed from five-gallon pails to smooth countertop to an electronic scale. He segregated random samples and carried them over to a magnifying light.

"They're good." Daniel hovered at his shoulder. "Quality control claims priority in my lab. It's right up there with cleanliness."

"You work in a barn." Basil examined the double-B butterfly logo on both sides of a lime green tablet. He felt Daniel's presence too close, the chemist's ego pushing into his personal space like a pocket of heated air. Arrogance could kill a man in their business. Basil gestured Daniel to take a step back.

"A very clean, former dairy barn. You're welcome to come inspect it." Daniel flicked lint off his black polo shirt.

"It had better keep that identity to the outside world." Basil moved a second visit to the lab outside of Crystal Springs, Wisconsin, up on his list of priorities. One more piece of evidence to support the rumor of Daniel ignoring his "exclusive" contract with Basil and the man would be hosting an angry instead of patient wholesaler.

"No problem. My parents buy the story I'm working on a better mouse poison."

Basil choked back a laugh. "And are you?"

"It would kill them. No doubt about it. One nibble or lick and a mouse, rat, even a cat or dog would be gone from heart failure."

"Is that what my customers can look forward to?" Basil scraped the edge of one dose with a clean knife and touched his tongue to the powder. No doubt about the quality of this batch. He reached for a bottle of water, rinsed his mouth, and spat into a trash can.

"You and I plus half the literate population know 'E' in all its forms causes problems in the long term. How many of your customers will live long enough for them to show? Or be able to trace it back?" Daniel took a casual stance with both thumbs hooked into his back pockets.

"All that reminiscing from my elders about 'wild in my younger days' is one reason I'm in this business." Basil smiled at Daniel. "And the money. A person can't ignore the positive financial aspect of pharmaceuticals."

"Easier to sleep when the pillow's full of cash."

"Speaking of payment." Basil unlocked a cabinet and pulled out a black sling pack. "The boys will pack up your transport pails with the usual raw materials."

Daniel opened the pouch and thumbed through random bundles of cash.

Basil gulped down the final third of his water and began a slow circuit of Daniel's truck. He peered behind the seats for any stray containers. "How many business appointments today?"

"Just the one." Daniel threaded a slim nylon tie to secure the money pack's zipper. "Why do you ask?"

Basil shrugged. "Color me curious." He paused at the rear left bumper, pointed with his toe. "Is this new?"

"What? The sticker?"

"Yeah. Who are the Cougars?" Basil studied the font of "Go Cougars" and the paw print done in bright yellow on green. The design and color combination pulled a cord in his memory that took only a few seconds to connect to a certain white van.

"Local high school sold those this spring."

The Crystal Springs mascot is the Cougars. Basil clicked a photo with his cell phone. "My little brother likes bumper stickers."

Chapter Five

Mona tucked the cash from Lorraine Terrier deep into her pocket. Today's work had been demanding enough to take her mind off the trio of Linc, Basil, and Matt for much of the time. In addition, Lorraine turned out to be talkative and informative. If Mona stayed in Eau Claire she'd return and work next week.

"Ready?" Linc reached for his seat belt.

"All set." She recited road signs and landmarks with silent lips during the late afternoon drive from the greenhouse to Linc's duplex. At every stop sign and traffic light she scanned for Basil's distinctive ride. A chill had lingered deep within her all day, a reminder of her status as prey. He could use a different car. She tensed and squeezed the shoulder belt.

"Home again," Linc announced before he pressed the garage door opener and guided the van inside.

Home? "Temporary."

"Your decision." He opened the driver's door. "One day? A week? It's up to you."

She stood beside the van and looked out the open double garage door. It would only take a moment to grab her pack and dart outside. And do what? Spend another night on campus evading security guards and their questions? Rent a motel room and dream of her money flying away?

Linc can be trusted. We've known him two years. Mona snatched the phrases from Lorraine's comments and hung on tight. She wanted to believe the other woman's assessment. Giving another person time and opportunity to show true colors came naturally to her. She lifted her backpack and scanned the space. Shelves filled most of one long wall. Stacks of baskets draped with tattered blankets sat in front of them.

"Hey. Everything okay?" Linc came around the rear of the van carrying the large magnetic sign from the driver's side.

"I'm good. I won't be running off today." She set her pack on an overturned plastic bucket near a small door. "Need a little help?"

"I won't turn it down." He placed the sign he carried face down on a shelf and gestured to the other magnetic sign still on the van. "It works best to start at a corner, and tap it with the side of your hand until you can get a couple of fingers behind it."

"Why are we taking them off?" She had noticed the panels with a bright green design similar to the business card on campus this morning. They'd been absent yesterday, she was sure of it—almost.

"Tomorrow's Saturday."

She shrugged and began to follow his directions for removing the magnetic sign. "It always follows Friday."

"I go to the orchard on the weekends. It's out of our service area. No need for the signs."

Orchard. Farm. She slid her forearm under the panel and held one end of the sign away from the van while Linc freed the other end. This must be the family land near that little town—Crystal Springs. She remembered a snatch of conversation mentioning a problem with either the orchard or the land. "Every weekend?"

"Almost." He moved toward her pulling the sign free. "You're invited. Or does Lorraine have plans for you?"

"Monday. She'll drive us from the greenhouse. Like today. Only earlier." Mona pressed her lips tight. If she remained. If Basil didn't find her. Best not to voice what she didn't want to happen.

"Figured as much. What did you attack today?"

She struggled not to smile at his word choice. It was close to the truth. "We started clearing out bedroom closets. She said her sister and brother-in-law moved into the house thirty-five years ago. From the looks of what we found today, I'll guess her relatives saved every receipt, utility bill, and pay stub they ever received."

"Maybe she can rent a heavy-duty shredder." Linc unlocked the entrance to the house proper and pressed the control for the garage door. "Ready to go inside?"

She snatched up her pack. "Do I get a full real-estate sales tour?"

"Condensed version." He stopped in a small foyer and removed his work boots. "Up six steps you'll find the main living area, kitchen, office, and a half bath. We'll go down first. That's ten steps to two bedrooms, full bath, laundry, and storage. Follow me."

She stayed two steps behind during the descent to an open area with washer and dryer visible and several closed doors. "Nice."

"My room. Off limits." He tapped a pale wood panel before opening the bathroom door and pointing inside.

She blinked back surprise at the huge, bright flowers on the shower curtain. She'd have guessed a solid neutral color was more his style.

"Your room." He opened the door next to the one he'd declared his own and gestured her forward.

Mona entered a generous room furnished with a bookcase and small table and chair, plus a metal framed futon. One window set high in the wall furnished light and a reminder they stood in a basement room. She dropped her pack on the floor and went to the window. With the sill at forehead height, she tipped her face up a few degrees to look out at trimmed grass and wooden steps leading to a deck. Worm's eye view. "This ... this is very nice." She realized he'd stepped away, listened for a moment, and heard a door hinge complain. "Linc?"

"I'm searching for the sheets that come closest to fitting your bed." He stepped into view with bedding and towels draped over one arm and a pillow dangling from his other hand.

"Thanks." In an instant she began to case the pillow. She allowed her gaze to loiter across his shoulders and arms while he pulled the futon away from the wall. He looked more luscious than a Chippendale's calendar man. It was time to move her thoughts off the male body an arm's length away before she said something foolish. "Nice room. Do you have guests often?"

"Family's stayed."

She picked up the towels and draped them over the chair back. Three children in a framed photo over the table caught her attention. "The kids in this photo ... which one are you?"

"The taller boy. That was taken a long time ago."

"So I figured." She glanced between the man switching the futon into bed configuration and the boy holding a fat, black puppy. Yes, she could see a resemblance between man and boy, as well as both boys and the girl in the photo. "Your brother and sister?"

"Madison, my sister, is currently a food scientist, wife, and mother." He walked over and leaned against a bit of wall near the door. "Jackson, the boy with the tooth missing in the photo, grew up to be an attorney."

"I …"

"Lawyers feast at the expense of the starving."

"I didn't say that." She looked at his smile. "I'll hold my tongue on the lawyer jokes."

"No one else does. Jackson tells them best."

She allowed a genuine smile to linger more than a heartbeat. The warmth and luck present here paralleled gatherings with her few longtime friends. At first peek, Linc's family appeared to be one that didn't take everything serious all the time. Not so very long ago, she, Matt, and mother could fill the apartment with laughter, showing off a new recipe or bargain wardrobe additions. She missed those days.

"Come on." Linc brushed her arm on his way out the door. "I'm getting hungry. I'll show you the kitchen. I've got work in the office to occupy me while you perform your cooking magic."

She stood still, fighting the urge to hold the warmed skin where he had touched her. How many months since she'd experienced a man's touch? Too long. My imagination's getting carried away. "It's talent and practice. No magic involved."

"Let me be the judge, will you? I haven't been grocery shopping for more than a week. For all I know, I'm out of all the key ingredients."

Twenty minutes later, Mona squirted a portion of dish detergent into the stream of hot water. Tension fled her body with every breath. Kitchens were familiar territory, and Linc's compact model, with the counter completing a large U and separating the workspace from the dining end of the great room, felt right. Even the pantry behind the narrow door in the hall fit the space.

She rinsed the dishes from her cooking preparation and allowed her mind to pick highlights from the day.

Today they'd gone over to the house on Polk Street. Lorraine had given her a few instructions on one bedroom closet and then gone to work in the next room. Exclamations and comments of disbelief punctuated through the slim wall dividing them. At the rate they discovered things today, the large Dumpster scheduled for delivery on Monday would be full in two days. And Linc's suggestion of a heavy-duty shredder was worth a mention. Over a simple lunch of tuna sandwiches, Lorraine sketched out portions of Linc's background. Two years ago he'd been working for a major seed company and looking for a job closer to Crystal Springs. Linc's mentor, a friend of Dr. Terrier, made a few calls at the right time and career matchmaking resulted.

Mona had shared a few of her ambitions in the restaurant field when Lorraine's questions turned in her direction. Lots of nods and follow-up questions made her feel as if lunch had ended with a preliminary job interview.

She glanced over the counter, past the dining table set for two, and out the patio door. A small wooden deck was attached to the house and doubled as a fire exit. She reached for the next dish and compared the scene outside the slider to the view from her bedroom. Half-basement, lower level, it gave a different perspective than past bedrooms.

He didn't need a housekeeper; that much was obvious from the general appearance of the place. Why had he taken her in as a stray? Why not set her up with a married couple? Or a single female who wanted to share rent? Friend or enemy? Either way I'll keep him close until I know.

"Hey. It smells good."

She pivoted at the sound of Linc's words.

"Whoa." He retreated a step and raised his arms in surrender.

"It'll be done in ten." She skimmed her gaze over him, amazed at how wide his eyes opened in a face pale with surprise.

"Put …" His throat showed the mechanics of swallowing. "Put down the weapon."

She glanced at her right hand. The eight-inch French chef knife shed a drop of soapy water. "Weapon? This?" She waited for his nod before slipping the kitchen tool into the sink of clear rinse water. "No problem. Better now?"

Linc rubbed his arms. "Much. Sorry about that."

Three steps closer and Mona stopped, rested her hips against the counter, and pointed to his right arm.

A previous glimpse had hinted at a scar but now she realized the length of it. "Is it because of that? How long ago?"

"January." He traced the long shiny scar with his left index finger. Silence descended upon them before he lowered his arms and stored them behind his back. "It's a complicated story. The summary is that I'm not good at disarming a woman with a knife. Can we save the details for later?"

"Later works for me." She understood the man in front of her well enough to know he disliked being forced on a topic. And she still needed to consider what to do if Basil traced her. Were his men trying to beat her location out of Matt? "What do you drink with supper?"

"Milk. Please."

She opened the fridge, found the milk, and filled a tall, clear glass for him. "I'll help myself to this iced tea. If you don't mind."

"Suit yourself."

A quarter of an hour later, Mona poked the last piece of elbow macaroni on her plate and raised her gaze to Linc. He'd been silent. Not even so much as a "good" or "poor" on the chicken breasts baked and smothered with commercial pasta sauce. "Am I hired?"

"As cook? Certainly. If you bother to look, you'll see my plate is empty."

If he expected her to stay he'd need to learn to talk. She wanted confirmation of some of Lorraine's statements before she spent the night with only a lightweight door between them. "Did you go to college here? In Eau Claire?"

He spooned the last of the pasta onto his plate. "They didn't have the major I wanted. I graduated from Stevens Point. They have a better horticulture program."

"Sounds like you've had a thing for plants for some time."

"That's one way to put it. Two years ago, when I wanted to change jobs, this was the best market close to the farm. Still is."

"I've never been on a farm. Does it have cows and pigs or only crops?" So far his answers remained consistent with her previous information. How could she keep him talking? Her knowledge of farming wouldn't fill a teaspoon. A visit to the Minnesota State Fair last year was as close as she'd been. Her companion, a co-worker recently arrived from a rural portion of northern Minnesota, tried several times during their hours at the fairgrounds to explain the difference between various breeds of livestock. But at the end of the day she remembered the displays of sewing, woodworking, and other crafts more clearly than the barns.

"The renter plants corn and soybeans. I go every weekend to work in the orchard. Five acres and the old hog shed are reserved in the lease agreement."

"Who lives there? Grandparents? An uncle?"

"A guy named Daniel Larson." He twisted his mouth as if he'd bitten into a lemon.

"From your expression I'll guess he's not a friend."

"He's a bully. Or at least that's how I've seen him since I was a kid. If you're lucky you won't meet him."

You're making me curious.

"My grandparents used to live in the house. It's known as Hilltop Farm. Decades ago an ancestor painted Hilltop across the end of the barn. When I get a few things straightened out I'll rename it Hilltop Orchard."

"Are your grandparents ...?"

"Gone? Yes. Grandmother died a year ago later this month. Gramps passed two years before. The estate rents the land. Until ... never mind, it gets complicated."

"Perhaps you'd rather save it for dessert. I put together peach shortcake."

His jaw slacked and he sent her a silent question. "I didn't have peaches in the house."

"I improvised with canned." I didn't find any fresh produce in the house.

"Oh. I'd forgotten."

She pushed her chair back and went to assemble the desserts. "I took it seriously when you told me to cook with what I found. Was that wrong?"

"No, not at all. We'll work in a trip to the supermarket on Sunday." He stacked their empty plates and transferred them to the counter. "Are you going to the farm with me? I can promise you hard work and fresh air. But it would be volunteer labor."

She pressed one peach slice into the crest of the whipped topping and pushed the bowl toward him. A plea for her company seemed to radiate off of him. She detected a trace of—desperation? Maybe it was sincerity. She gave a quick check to the safety level and hoped her body language didn't reveal how much she feared Basil finding her in Eau Claire. "Lunch included?"

* * *

Basil sent the waitress a quick smile and pushed his empty iced tea glass toward the end of the table. "What time did you say you got off?"

"Don't bother with the pick-up lines, young man. My husband's a boxing instructor." The new night-shift server at Hiawatha's Griddle wore confidence and a name tag saying "Maggie." In an instant she settled his platter of eggs, sausage patties, and hash browns on the center of the paper placemat.

"Message received." He lifted two fingers in a salute before digging into his meal.

For the second night in a row Matt's sister was absent from her previous workplace. He'd ordered a two-minute beating by his top prison contact on the chance Matt would give up either her location or a trail to the money. The odds on either point were against Basil, but he'd lose credibility and power unless he tried. More and more the situation emerged as if Matt had been the object of one of the new members' jealousy. Soon he'd clean the riff-raff out of his own organization.

Matt's sister, Mona, sure was a pretty little thing. She improved the scenery in the diner with efficient movements, a cheerful attitude, and pure black hair he longed to push his fingers through. Where had she gone? Milwaukee? Chicago? A little crossroads town? A hunch deep in his core told him she was close. The bumper sticker pointed to Crystal Springs. Or an alumnus of the high school. Pity his contact at the DMV had suffered a gallbladder attack and underwent surgery before he could trace the van's plate.

"Joel, I'm not going to tell you politely again. The men's room needs attention." Maggie spoke loud enough to be heard above the clink of flatware two booths away.

Basil spread strawberry jam on rye toast and watched the busboy. He certainly fit Nick's description of the rogue dealer: slight build, no more than early twenties, and a bright blond faux mohawk. All Basil needed now was a few minutes alone and confirmation of what drugs the boy carried.

According to the large clock over the kitchen pass-through Basil had plenty of time. Joel left at five thirty on the dot. Thirty minutes gave Basil opportunity to enjoy his meal before he'd meet Joel out back.

As he sipped his tea he reviewed the conversation with Daniel today. His chemist was cheating him. He could feel it in the little lies about traffic delays and hesitation before answers. Maybe after a few minutes with Joel he could prove it. If the punk kid working in the diner carried tablets with Basil's logo he'd have enough evidence.

Half an hour later Basil stood in the shadows and observed the busboy step into the alley behind the restaurant. He waited until Joel cleared the Dumpster before stepping forward. "Hey, punk."

"Who?" An instant later Joel pivoted and sprinted toward the light on the corner.

Basil tackled him midway between Dumpster and the edge of the building. "Skittish. Acting guilty before I get the first question out. Not good form."

"You got no reason—"

"Show me your goods." Basil pulled the young man to his feet and twisted one arm behind his back. An instant later he caught the other wrist before it could touch him and wrapped an old leather shoelace around both wrists.

"Don't—"

"Save the denial for the cops. You were sweating buckets in chilly air less than ten minutes ago. Now tell me which pocket has your stash." He pushed Joel toward the brick wall. "Now."

"Ba ... back. My right."

"See, that wasn't hard." Basil pulled out a small plastic bag and held it up to the light. "Hmmm. Three colors. Size matches. Want to bet on the logo?"

"I ... I ... bought those fair and square."

"Wrong answer." Basil pocketed the drugs and shoved Joel's shoulder against the building.

"You're no cop."

"Never claimed to be. Dealer's name."

Joel kicked out and twisted free of Basil's single arm hold.

"Bad move, Junior." Basil ducked and reached for the smaller man. "Mind your manners. Where?"

"Not your business." Joel worked free of the wrist binding and dropped into a squat. He glanced at the street only a short dash away and back to Basil's tattooed arm.

"It is now. Those are my trademark." Basil reached for Joel with his left hand and swung with his right fist. The shock wave when he connected with Joel's jaw went all the way to his collarbone.

Joel shook his head before lowering it and charging.

Basil moved aside fast enough to suffer only a glancing blow. He fisted both hands and pursued the younger man. Half of Basil's blows connected but that proved to be sufficient. "Who?" He panted. "Where?"

Joel crumpled against the steel trash bin. Blood trickled from both his nose and mouth.

"Exclusive distribution." Basil planted his feet shoulder width apart and stared down at the busboy. "My boys haven't sold to you for three weeks. Who's your new dealer?"

"Don't. No more." Joel wiped his face and managed to smear blood to new places on his cheek.

"Time's wasting."

Joel found the corner of the Dumpster and started to pull himself up. "No name."

"Description will do." Real names were rare in this business anyway.

"Tall. Thin."

"More." Basil stared into Joel's eyes, daring him to lie.

"A nice dresser. Gentleman. Unlike you."

Basil punched him in the solar plexus for the insult. "Where? When?"

"Today. Last week."

Basil added another hit to the side of Joel's face. He warmed with satisfaction as a new stream of blood formed at the corner of the busboy's mouth. "Where?"

"Loring."

"Damn him." Basil spit on Joel's foot at the name of a popular park. Police patrols had concentrated on the area for the last two weeks. It was reckless to conduct business there. "His ride?"

"Black." Joel retreated to the corner and swayed between wall and trash container. "Lots of chrome. Wisconsin plates."

Figures. Basil jerked Joel forward, delivered two more solid blows, and stood quietly as the busboy slipped into unconsciousness.

Chapter Six

Mona ran down the sidewalk in the eerie green light of an approaching storm. The bus on the corner. If I can get to it in time I'll be safe. Why aren't people moving? She dodged around a standing pedestrian. Before her foot was down again she was pulled backward, one arm around her neck and another at her waist. "No. No." She flailed her legs as she was lifted off the ground.

"Pay me." The man's lips brushed against her ear.

She glanced down and saw stars—a dozen or more—tattooed on the arm below her chin. Basil. Only he displayed that much gang rank, history, and privilege.

She flung her free arm back and hit—metal?

Mona curled her fingers around a smooth rod and opened her eyes. She clutched a portion of futon frame. It was a dream. A nightmare. Soft light seeped into the room from behind her and she began to see shapes. A door with a chair propped under the knob reminded her she was at Linc's apartment. And he was—she touched the wall—mere feet away. For a full minute she lay still, listening for something familiar, until the soft hum of highway traffic reached her ears. She snuggled under the blanket, comforted by the idea she was not alone in this new place.

Am I safe? Memory of the flashes in the parking garage raised a batch of gooseflesh. Basil commanded men. Controlled resources. Could he track Linc's van? The question made a good case to leave, find a bus headed to Madison or Milwaukee.

"Then?" she whispered. What next? Any job worth having would require ID. The further away she went, the more her Minnesota non-driver card would become memorable. Try to double back? Find a trucker willing to take her past the Twin Cities and drop her in a different part of Minnesota?

A yawn prodded her to close her eyes. She muttered a simple prayer from childhood, adding a petition for Matt's safety and her mother's soul. Without a conscious decision she reached out to rest her fingertips against the wall.

The man sleeping on the other side became more complex in each conversation. What sort of man talked of apples, land, and college classes late into the evening? At times he appeared to be giving her his biography. What did it matter to her that his first job for pay was walking dogs at his father's veterinary practice? She'd be gone from here soon.

I'll puzzle it all out later. She drew a deep breath and drifted into sleep.

"Hey. Sleeping Beauty." Linc's voice and two sharp knocks against the door cracked Mona's thin shell of sleep. "Time to get going."

Mona snapped her eyes open. White textured ceiling filled her line of sight. "I hear you."

"Dress in long pants and sleeves if you're coming to the farm."

Farm. Orchard. She turned toward the window and blinked in soft morning light leaking in around the mini-blinds. Had she overslept? "Got it."

She scrambled out of bed and pulled jeans, tank top, and clean underwear from her pack. If he so much as touched the doorknob she'd scream. A shiver disturbed her skin, reminding her of the struggle in her dream. I don't have time. This is a new day. She cut off the internal words before the conclusion of that family saying could form. She'd take today's ration of problems as they arrived, not seek them ahead of time.

Five minutes later she followed the scent of frying bacon up the steps. Some cook she was turning out to be. She fixed one decent supper and didn't even arrive in the kitchen first to make morning coffee. "Sorry I'm late. Need a hand?"

"I've got breakfast under control." Linc ladled pancake batter onto a large electric griddle.

She paused, soaking in the view. He moved with ease, picking up a bright red coffee mug for a sip while the pancakes turned golden. Over paint-spattered jeans he wore a dress shirt with an ink-stained pocket and the sleeves rolled up past the elbow. She glanced down and noticed thick gray socks. The sight of him stirred her more than either the coffee or bacon.

"Sleep okay?" He flipped the first of four pancakes.

"I guess so. Didn't intend to sleep in or disrupt your morning routine."

"What routine? Help yourself to coffee. I'm almost done here."

* * *

"That sounds painful." Linc glanced again at Mona's profile. He'd managed to dig up enough questions to keep her talking for most of the forty-plus miles this morning. He figured he could listen to her for hours. Tonight, over ice cream on the deck, he'd have to ask more about her Chinese grandparents.

"You asked for my worst experience on my bike. Getting caught in hail, even for a few minutes, was memorable. The end result turned out to be only a few bruises and a tattered poncho." She sighed. "City adventures are the only kind I've had."

"People can move. Have new experiences in a different setting." Will you change for me? Learn to love land and apple trees? He cleared his throat and put on the tourist guide hat. "We'll pass two signs almost at our turn. The first one is the official village limits marker with the population. The second, to entice travelers off the road, claims we're the 'Heart of a Peaceful Valley.' Local joke is that the valley's so peaceful as to be comatose."

"It can't be … population 522? That's …"

"Tiny." He turned from the federal highway onto a village street. "High school is on our right. Newer elementary building will be on the left past the park. Basketball and baseball are the sports of choice."

"Home of the Cougars." She read the proclamation on the side of the building. "How can such a small place have a high school?"

"Outlying farms. It's a big school district in square miles." He checked his mirrors to confirm he wasn't blocking traffic and pulled to a stop on the narrow shoulder. "Springs in the park back a hundred yards give the place the name. Years ago someone with ambition enlarged a small natural pool at the base. The creek leading out from it isn't much at first but grows considerable after several more join in at the other end of town."

"Looks pleasant."

He studied her for a long moment and then eased the van forward. "Majority of the locals are friendly. You won't be the only visitor this weekend. Only the prettiest."

"Flatterer." She flashed her brief, warm smile with the word.

He pulled into a gravel parking strip in front of a long, metal building. Three round grain bins poked up behind the roofline, part of the animal feed mixing facilities. "I've got business here at Farm Service before we go up the hill. Do you want to come in?"

She gave the building and mud-spattered pick-up parked on the other side of the entrance a quick look before turning her gaze across the street. "I don't think so. That store, Harter's Essentials, do they sell sunglasses? I forgot to pack mine."

"Best possibility in town. I know they carry bottled drinks. Could you get us each one? We have a water tap available for refills. By the way, no bathroom at the orchard."

"Thanks." She slammed the passenger door.

"Do you have money?" He exited the van and called to her back.

"Enough."

Linc stood for a minute, puzzling if the force on the door translated as anger or merely a stiff hinge resisting her small stature. Petite. The women in his life kept reminding him to use the more flattering term. No matter the word, Mona filled a pair of jeans better than most. Watching her cross the street was an enjoyable activity. Go inside and get your spray.

"Morning, Corey." Linc greeted one of Hilltop's neighbors.

"Must be Saturday if you're in town. What's going on with you this weekend?"

"Routine spraying." Linc turned to Sam, the clerk. "Did my order come in? Five gallons of the NAA."

Sam promised to check and disappeared through swinging saloon-style doors.

"Had ourselves a nice rain midweek." Corey launched into a pleasant monologue which included the readings on his rain gauge and complaints about a road construction detour adding five miles to his window factory job commute.

Linc inserted a word or two where appropriate and studied the neighbor a dozen years his senior. Corey tended toward the colorful side of the personality scale. He'd talk to anyone with a pulse when he was sober. But when he started drinking—every night off from the factory—he got quiet with a trace of malice. The only other habit setting him apart from most happened to be his walks—he called them rambles—down access lanes or across fields.

"A man can always trust you to have a pulse on activities up on the hill." Linc rested one hip against the counter while Corey described the newest litter of kittens in his machine shed. A moment later the man launched into comments about his wife's conversion of the garage into a dance studio.

"I don't understand Patti's enthusiasm for teaching dance." Corey smiled a bit as he spoke his wife's name. "Only a few of the old style halls are still in operation. But she seems to think she can build a demand."

"Hey, Sam," Linc called to the clerk. "Has that spray I ordered gone into hiding?"

"Give me a few." Sam's words drifted to the sales area.

"As I was saying, you ever want a kitten, or two, or three, you stop by. Don't have the heart ... Well, looky here." Corey hooked his thumbs behind his black suspenders and grinned. "If it isn't Mr. Dance Student? Morning, neighbor."

Linc turned his gaze to Daniel Larson striding toward the counter. Daniel lived in the house at Hilltop in a gesture of independence from his parents, who lived a mile away and rented the land. Still walks like a bully. Linc had been a target of Daniel's pranks and insults since his first summer visits to the farm. "Morning. How are things at Hilltop?"

Daniel tugged the brim of his Pioneer Seed Corn cap to acknowledge Corey and turned to Linc. "Man who actually cared would check for himself on more than weekends."

"I need the day job." Linc kept his voice light. "At least for now."

"Time's running out for you."

Linc moved his gaze over Daniel and wondered if he knew the particulars of the will from his parents or only the plentiful local gossip. "I've got a plan." She's buying drinks and sunglasses.

"That's an old story. What was that girl's name? Tami? Understand she left you and your apple trees. Pardon me while I take her side. God didn't create a messier tree in all the world." Daniel set his feet at shoulder width and crossed his arms in imitation of a bar bouncer with indigestion.

"You know better than to trust the local rumors." Tami's sudden exit from Linc's life, three weeks before their scheduled wedding, had nothing to do with apple trees. It involved a software engineer with a low bar on the morality scale offering a ticket to California. And Linc wore a scar on his arm illustrating the feelings in their parting. But this was neither the time nor place to set the record straight.

"Fact." Daniel jabbed a finger toward Linc. "Time is not your friend. End of this summer, I'll be ripping out your stupid trees and painting over the sign on the barn."

"Don't buy the paint yet." Linc pushed away from the counter, clenched his fists, and advanced one step. Living in the farmhouse didn't give Daniel the right to threaten his trees. Eleven days remained for Linc to marry and claim the property. Eleven whole days left to lay claim to the entire 240 acres: buildings, water well, and orchard. All he had to do—too much to waste time and breath with Daniel.

"Hey, Sam," Daniel called out as he stepped forward until his worn loafers were toe to toe with Linc's Red Wing work boots. "How much Classic Barn Red you got in stock?"

Linc flexed his hands once, twice, and felt the heat of anger run up his neck. "Time's not up."

"Don't matter. I'm going to enjoy the look on your face when I sign the deed." Daniel's hands shot out against Linc's shoulders.

Linc stumbled backward. His arms slashed air and he stayed on his feet. In a heartbeat his right hand opened and slapped against Daniel's cheek. "I said, time's not up."

"End of the month I'll buy the whole damn place."

"With what?" Linc eased back as Corey stepped up and touched each of them on the chest as a signal to separate. "Do you hold a great 'chemistry' patent? You've killed or scared off all the cats. Even the stray dog hanging around in March has disappeared." He stared into Daniel's cold brown eyes. "You making ink and printing money in the barn?"

"Whoa, boys." Corey stiffened his arms to get the pair further apart. "Let's cool this off a bunch."

"Spoiled little city creep. He can't even throw a good fist." Daniel looked over Linc's shoulder toward the swinging doors.

"Got the spray ..." Sam spoke behind Linc.

"Good." Linc pulled out his wallet and handed a credit card to the clerk without blinking or taking his stare off Daniel. "Mr. Larson was just about to explain his recent wealth."

"Nothing of the sort."

"New trucks don't grow on trees." Linc fought back a grin. "Apples do."

Daniel picked up one foot before Corey stepped between the men and faced Daniel. "Not here. Not now."

"Thanks, neighbor." Linc turned his attention to Sam while he gathered his receipt and picked up the five-gallon can of thinning spray. Angry energy bubbled under his skin while his brain took Corey's advice about the time and place. He managed enough manners to raise one hand in farewell to Sam and Corey on his way to the door.

"You owe me an explanation, Mr. Larson. Why has your truck been at my place three nights this week? Late. On nights Patti doesn't schedule dancing class." Corey's voice continued with questions and accusations about dance lessons and Corey's wife until the door blocked the sound.

* * *

Mona sat on the van's floor, her feet on the gravel lot outside the open side door. Sparse traffic rolled past, half of the vehicles pulling into the gas pumps at the store she'd recently left. Nine o'clock and the day loomed full of promise. A polite clerk, tidy restroom, and the usual convenience store items, including new sunglasses, encouraged her to visit the store again.

Stop it. By next weekend I'll be long gone.

She glanced again at the Farm Service store. Should she go inside? No, the utilitarian sign and entrance indicated a male-dominated place, best saved for another day.

Instead she turned her attention to the other vehicles in the parking lot. Two pick-up trucks were parked side by side, a study in contrasts. The one nearest the door wore faded red paint, a dent in the tailgate, and a skirt of fine mud spatters. Less than three feet away a black truck with bright chrome shined in the morning sun. Matt and his friends called vehicles like that "flash" and bragged of owning one in the future. Basil drives flash. She rubbed her arms as a mental image of the unique red vehicle chilled her bones.

Linc emerged from the store at that moment, walking unevenly as he carried a large bucket with colorful warning labels. He tugged his Brewers cap down against the sunshine and clipped out two words. "Side door."

"Yes, sir." She stepped aside, confusion flipping her stomach at his change in demeanor from a friendly smile when he walked into the building.

He braced the pail between the side of the van and a piece of lumber on the rubber mat. An instant later he slammed the door shut and pointed her into the passenger seat without a word.

"I won't bite." He broke the tense silence after they passed two more side streets. "My problem's not connected to you."

"Okay." She wasn't the sort to argue. Not when he was her only transportation in a town that looked as if a Greyhound would be a novelty. She stayed silent, her attention on the street and business signs as they continued past a mixture of brick and frame buildings. They turned when a rather new, large, low building blocked their way.

"Local Care Center." He pointed. "County health department runs various clinics out of the smaller building across their main parking lot."

"I'll remember that." She made the sign of the cross when they paused at the stop sign in front of St. Mathias Roman Catholic Church.

An unintelligible word from Linc captured her attention.

"Problem?" She leaned forward to glimpse more than his profile.

"Hope not."

Mona studied the determined set to his mouth. "I can see you have questions. Yes, I come from a Catholic family. Grandmother was very devout. Me? Not so much, but I'd check the box on any questionnaire."

He sighed and his shoulders shed their stiff control of a moment before.

"Do you have a rule against devout Catholic housekeepers?"

"No. Just mark me as surprised. I never hired a housekeeper before you—saint or sinner."

She turned her gaze to the passing scenery, cataloging the variety of styles in the houses. Her religion, even if she lacked an obvious one, was no concern to him. It was private; she didn't have plans to preach.

"The farm, Hilltop, is three point six miles from the hardware store." Linc's voice returned to the tourist guide tone from earlier. "Good county road until the driveway. If all goes well, I'll get a load or two of gravel on that before winter comes around."

"Nice first impression for a small town. Do they have a café on the other long street?"

"Yes. Front Street is home to Sunrise Café, the bank, fire department, and a few other shops. Street plan resembles a ladder. Front and Back, connected with rungs named after trees."

"Sounds simple."

"No one uses the street names. You'll hear references like 'the old Anderson place' or 'turn at the barber shop' most of the time."

"Is it nice? The café?" Do they need a waitress or a cook? She gave her head an invisible slap for thinking about the staff at a business in a tiny village she probably would never set foot in after today.

"We won't be eating there. They close mid-afternoon, after the lunch crowd. Our sandwiches will need to tide us over until later. I usually stop at Jack's for supper." He glanced toward her. "That's Jack's Village Tavern. Any objections?"

"I've been inside a variety of taverns." Her best paying jobs had been at sports bars. She could use one of those in the near future—the job and the tips—not the long, irregular hours.

"We've arrived. Almost."

They turned onto a narrow strip of gravel and slowed to little more than walking speed between a large red barn on her left and a two-story frame house with a screen porch facing the road. "Who did you say lives in the house?"

"Renter. Daniel Larson."

She settled her gaze on him while his mouth wavered between a frown and neutral. Last night Linc called Daniel a bully. She imagined an unwashed, unshaved, bald creature akin to the occasional homeless she passed in the city.

"Welcome to Hilltop Orchard." Linc stopped the van with the nose close to a steel gate.

"I'll get it." Mona exited the van in record speed and unfastened the latch, a short chain with a dog leash end.

"Open is fine." He parked between two rows of young trees.

She gazed down the nearest line of slender trees hugging a tall wire fence. They went on for—a football field? And they were baby trees, with bushy little green tops not much taller than Linc. The scene in front of her and the orchard she'd visited with friends two years ago didn't look alike at all. This reminded her of—she dug into memories of textbook photos—a vineyard, with trees instead of grapevines. "How many?"

"Sixteen rows times a hundred and twenty. Give or take. It's only a beginning."

She studied the grass against her sneakers and eavesdropped on a sparrow conversation. After a long moment she raised her gaze to his face. Linc's dream, the orchard he'd spoken of with pride, stretched out in front of her. Half or more of the enclosed rectangle remained bare except for wild grass, or ground cover, or whatever. This place, with pale new leaves indicating the presence of a breeze, surrounded them raw and unformed. The only thing with less substance was the future restaurant she carried around in her head.

"Come on." He opened the rear van doors. "I'll introduce you to the tool shed and you can help me put these things where they belong."

She hung her new sunglasses on her tank top as soon as she emptied her arms. The shed, even with half of the wide door open, stayed dim, the air scented with dirt and oil. A small tractor, a shallow wagon, and implements she couldn't name claimed the majority of the floor space. Shelves with a variety of strange metal and wood tools, baskets nested up to her shoulder, and half a dozen red gas cans lined the edges.

"This is our water source." Linc reached over a metal vat and turned a single tap. "It runs clean and cold after a minute or two. Have you ever used a trimmer?"

"Landscape? Grass?" She waited for his nod. "Once. A friend demonstrated an electric on a long cord."

"Then allow me to introduce to you his gas-powered big brother." He shut off the water and removed one of the tools from the bottom shelf.

Mona wrapped one hand around a molded handle and her other around a metal cane protruding from a third of a lawn mower. This didn't look like an acquaintance, let alone brother, to any yard tool she'd used. She stood still, waiting for instructions while Linc sorted through a small bin.

"You need gloves. Give me another minute to find a left small the mice haven't attacked. We used to have enough cats on the place to keep small rodents in check. Damn Daniel and his chemistry experiments." He shook out a second brown glove and forced the pair into her hand supporting the wand. "We'll gas it up outside. Better add the other shirt."

A few moments later Mona folded the cuffs back and over on the worn dress shirt Linc had loaned her. It still gave her complete arm coverage. She pulled on the gloves and picked up the trimmer again.

"Hold it straight." Linc inserted a funnel and poured fuel into a plastic tank. "The cans are numbered. Always use number two for the trimmer. It's a two-cycle."

"Got it." She understood that two cycle and four-cycle motors used different fuel but could not at the moment remember why. Or which one you added the oil to.

"We'll get you started trimming around these younger trees. Then I'll mix my spray and begin with the older ones."

She lifted the tool and sent him a smile of false confidence.

"Here. You'll need these in a few minutes." He draped protective earmuffs over her wrist.

"Pull this to start?" Mona jerked the cord. Silence from the trimmer. "Again?" Another false start later she fought to temper the vibration that swept up her arms.

Linc stood behind her. Close. Very close. His arms formed a loose circle around hers, his fingertips resting on the backs of her hands as he guided the spinning string at her feet in an arc around a trellis post. "Higher. Steady. Back a little. Let the end of the line do the work."

Easy for you to say. She took a small step to the right and blinked behind safety goggles over sunglasses as the head of the trimmer expanded every move of her arms, cutting right up to the edge of the wooden post. A little confidence seeped in when Linc retreated half a step. She moved in slow, cautious steps along the route he indicated.

"Turn it off." He pointed to the switch.

She pressed her lips tight and waited for the engine noise to fade. "Something wrong?"

"Not at all. Put on the ears and start up again. I'll watch a bit and then you're on your own."

Within half an hour Mona controlled her own space with new sureness. Fresh grass fell along the wire and around young apple trees at her command. Tension and sunshine combined to heat her back and legs. These trees, the youngest row, were her size, not intimidating like thick maple and ash in city parks. Their delicate leaves brushed against her head when she got close. She risked a glance at Linc. He worked half a dozen rows away, moving a spray wand over a tree crown and then quickly moving on to the next.

She paused after the next tree to enjoy the sight of fair-weather clouds in a summer sky and to savor the scent of growing leaves mixed with the fresh-cut grass in the air. City noises and scents seemed a world apart. Basil would never find her here. Crystal Springs would be the perfect place to hide if a person could solve the problem of an income. Pity her stay would be temporary.

* * *

Linc recharged the backpack sprayer and squinted toward the sun to estimate the time as he neared the end of the second row. He'd been spraying more than an hour, and should be able to complete another row before taking a break. The trimmer buzzed at the northern edge of the trees, a constant reminder he didn't work alone today. He shifted the weight on his back and glimpsed Mona moving between the slender trunks. Get to work. Find words and remember them.

As he finished spraying the second tree in the next row he noticed a vehicle coming up the drive.

Daniel. The charitable thing to do would be to wave the renter over and offer an apology for giving him a slap in Farm Service this morning. Linc held a very short internal debate and decided to let the other man make the first move to patch up the tiff. After all, Daniel had started today's incident with verbal taunts and a shove.

Linc lifted the spray wand and circled it over the crown of the next tree.

Daniel got out of his truck and looked toward the orchard. A moment later, without a wave or called greeting, he turned and walked to the barn.

With a shrug, Linc moved along the row. Daniel claims he's going to buy this place? Linc thought about all the different ways he'd calculated a purchase if he didn't fulfill the marriage clause of the will. Two hundred and forty acres, house, barn, and sheds came to more than any of the three banks he'd talked to would lend. He did have savings. They came from living like a monk during five years with the seed company plus a little from a great-aunt.

What did Daniel have for assets? He'd either dropped or flunked out of college after two years. Since then he'd worked several short-term construction jobs. The last three years he'd spent farming with his father and grandfather. Maybe he was printing money. Linc would run the possibility past Daryl the next time he spoke with the retired Secret Service agent.

The trimmer went silent and he turned to look for Mona. She stood beside one of his youngest Honey Crisp trees and put the water bottle to her lips. Good. It's getting hot. Heat, not from the sun, flooded his neck. Get back to work. He sighed and took his own advice.

Thinning spray emerged as a dribble instead of a mist and Linc reached for the handle to recharge the sprayer. No familiar slosh of liquid as he changed position. He pulled a bright orange strip of cloth from his pocket and fastened it to the trellis, marking his starting point. As he walked along the row toward the shed he spotted Mona guiding the trimmer, her posture signaling attention to her work. A bubble of pleasure swelled in his chest at the sight of her figure in jeans and an oversized shirt concentrating on a task. He tried to imagine her face. *How will it change if—when—I ask her to stay?*

Every few trees this morning he'd tested and discarded opening lines. If his awkward words had the substance of pruned shoots, the stack would be the size of the tool shed going toward the volume of the old dairy barn. *Do you have a boyfriend? I was engaged once. Would you help me with a problem?* He shook his head at the neediness in the final one. It would be suited for a whining preschooler, not a man of twenty-nine proposing to a charming, if new, acquaintance.

Tires crunched on gravel and he looked toward the driveway. He smiled at the black sedan and hurried to meet his friend at the orchard entrance.

"Hey. I didn't expect to see you today." Linc set his protective mask and vinyl gloves on a tarp beside the empty sprayer.

"You know how to arouse my curiosity." Daryl Frieberg met Linc with an extended hand. "I figured you'd be working in the orchard today. Is that Ms. Smith?"

"She wants to be called Mona. Wait here." Linc marched past the van and the support posts anchoring the long trellis to the row where she worked.

Mona pressed the trimmer switch and pushed off the protective ear muffs when Linc got her attention from the other side of the wire. "What's up?"

"We've got company."

She leaned the tool against the trellis and pulled off her gloves. "Is it good or bad?"

"The guest? He's a friend of mine. A complete opposite of your non-friend Basil."

She pulled off her hat and sent her hair into motion. It fell loose to her shoulders without a hint of the band which held it in a ponytail earlier this morning. "A break sounds good. What time is it?"

"A quarter to lunch." He shortened his steps to match her pace as they went to meet Daryl. He both cursed and blessed the fence between them in silence. Little flecks of grass in her hair begged him to reach out, brush them away, and test the texture of the strands. Then he'd take a finger, just one, and skim it across her lower lip where she'd applied lip gloss early this morning.

Too soon they reached the end of the row and he introduced her to Daryl.

"I've known Lincoln all his life." Daryl gestured them to sit on the tarp as if he hosted the meeting. "His dad and I tormented the teachers together from first grade through college applications."

Mona propped the trimmer against the shed and eased down on the tarp into a perfect tailor position. "So you're the one who knows his secrets?"

"I also know which ones not to share."

"That's even more important."

Linc retrieved the lunch cooler from the van and listened to the casual banter between the others. Daryl squatted, keeping his attention on Mona with the exception of a quick occasional glance.

"Is there any corner of the country you've not lived in, Mr. Freiberg?"

Daryl stood, brushed invisible dirt from his black dress pants, and gave her an asymmetrical smile. "I've only lived in six states and DC. All the other places were mere visits, a few weeks at most."

"Sounds exciting to me. Until recently I'd not set foot out of Minnesota."

"Well, I've taken enough of your time. Don't want to impede progress in the orchard and all that. However, you are invited to supper. Kathy and I will pick up the tab at Jack's. Agreed?"

"That's the tavern in town," Linc reminded Mona. "We'd be in for excellent pizza and a variety of beers. If you're so inclined."

She nodded. "Pizza is good. After this heat a beer will hit the spot."

"Good. What time, Linc?"

He shrugged, glanced at Mona, and decided to go early rather than late. "Five thirty?"

"See you then. We might even be ahead of the thunderstorm in the forecast."

* * *

"You have interesting friends." Mona stood in the tool shed doorway drinking water after Daryl drove away. "Do you have any of your own generation?"

"A few." Linc finished washing his hands under the cold water tap. "My classmates and I scattered, followed the jobs. Or did you mean face-to-face friends?"

She rested her head against the smooth wood of the door frame and watched him in shadow dry his hands and fill a water bottle. Intriguing. Too tempting. She discovered breathing became easier when she looked away from the actual man and gazed at his thin white coveralls on the grass beside the sprayer. At the moment they reminded her of a deflated Christmas decoration. "In my case they're the same."

"I'll have to broaden your horizons."

"You already have." She walked over to the cooler and sat down. She remained aware of his gaze as he left the shed. With a blink and silent plea to the sky she conquered the urge to look at him. The more she looked, the more she wanted to touch. And if previous brief contact was any indication her hands would stay on him longer than their short acquaintance warranted. "Did you pack this before I came upstairs? What did you find?"

"Very basic peanut butter and strawberry jam. You can thank my mother for the jam when you meet her."

Mona's hand hovered over the top sandwich bag. Meet your mother? She must have heard wrong; his parents lived in West Allis, next to Milwaukee, hundreds of miles away. Did she miss a comment about a visit? She worked moisture into her throat. "I'm sure it's delicious."

"It is. Plentiful too. She's gotten most of the backyard into berries now."

"Is that where you get it? The plant thing? From her?"

"Hard to say." He ripped plastic off a sandwich and took a bite. "The garden at home interested me a little. But when we came to visit the farm I never wanted to leave. I guess Grandmother put in a good word or two because soon I was staying for two weeks per summer and then the entire school break."

"Did your grandfather have cows then?"

He nodded and swallowed. "He sold the herd when I was seventeen. His arthritis and a bad winter forced it. He continued with the crops until almost the end."

"So he knew about the orchard?"

"We fenced it off and planted the first eight rows together."

The number was double that now. She recalled his numbers of rows and trees from this morning and calculated out to almost 2000. Estimate, it depended on how large his give or take ended up. Any way you looked at it, a lot of trees grew on these acres and there was still plenty of empty space inside the fence. "I enjoy cooking with apples. Last fall I tweaked an apple crisp recipe well enough to get an 'excellent' on it in class."

Linc concentrated on his lunch as if it were a defense against further conversation.

I bragged again. She licked a drop of jam off a finger and stared off into the orchard. She could almost picture ripe apples, as large as her fist, among mature leaves in September.

"Mona." Linc broke the elongated silence. "I need to talk to you about my problem with the farm."

"Can you buy it from the estate? You did say the family owned it."

"That's the problem."

"My backpack is not full of money. If it were ..." She blinked back the tears that threatened when she thought too much about the medical bills and her mother's final days.

"You have your own bills." He completed her response. "No, the problem is, the way my grandparents wrote their will. I can only inherit the farm if I'm married."

She lowered the water bottle before it reached her lips. Her fingers curled tight around the plastic.

"Within eleven days."

What? She listened to her heart skip a beat, like a kettle of water the instant before a boil. "Who?" Mona gazed down at her hand clenching her drink. "Who is this girl you're going to marry?"

I'll leave as soon as we get back to Eau Claire. She made scrambled mental plans to ask for a ride to the bus depot. She had enough money for a ticket to put distance between her and a man less than two weeks away from his wedding.

"You. I hope. Will you marry me, Mona?"

She stared at him while her breathing suspended. Then, with an exhale and a blink, the scene spread before her as if she stood on the roof of the shed, observing. His hand reached out and gently enclosed hers. The warmth of his touch prompted another little hesitation in her heart. Will I ever breathe normally again?

"It needs to be a legal marriage. Which means the decision needs to be soon—Wisconsin has a waiting period. It doesn't have to be ... ah ... real."

She managed to lift her gaze from the tarp to meet his face. Words wobbled inside her throat and she licked her lips to gain time. "A marriage of convenience?"

"Yes." His Adam's apple bounced around like an elevator with all the buttons pushed at once. "A public marriage. In private ... no sex required."

Mona's neck heated until she felt certain it glowed like a toaster element. "Why? Why me?"

"We get along." He circled a thumb on the back of her hand. "At least it seems like we could."

She glanced down at their hands, checking for scorch marks. "How long have you known? About the deadline."

"Since the will was read." He tipped his head back as if the right words would be written in the sky. "Conditions require I be legally married one year from the date of Grandmother's death to take possession. Otherwise ..."

"And you waited until now?" She jerked her hand away and tucked it behind her.

He shook his head. "I was engaged before Granny died. When things settled after the funeral and harvest and everything, Tami agreed to Valentine's Day."

Tami?

He turned his arm and ran his index finger down the length of the prominent scar. "Parting gift. Three weeks before the wedding. Everything exploded in an argument on her way out the door to California with a software engineer."

She swallowed hard, remembered his pale face and arms up in surrender. "Explains your reaction to the knife yesterday."

"We could be friends. I feel that much deep down. Will you marry me?"

Mona settled the water bottle next to the cooler. Since she was a little girl sitting on her mother's lap listening to Cinderella she'd fantasized marriage proposals. Not one of those hundreds resembled the last few minutes. They'd never been on a date. Nor seen a movie together. Nor discussed New England versus Manhattan clam chowder.

"I'll ask Jackson, my lawyer brother, to draw up a pre-nup if you want."

If I want. She didn't know what she wanted. At the moment she doubted she could answer a simple question. Don't even think about a decision that would affect the rest of her life. If she had even a sliver of confidence in her body she'd stand and run away—follow the road to Crystal Springs, find Daryl Frieberg, and beg for—for what? "I'll think on it."

"How long?"

How long will I think? She saw desperation on his face and compassion flooded her chest. All her preconceived notions of relationships and marriage collided with his pleading, gray eyes. "Can you spare forty-eight hours?"

Chapter Seven

Mona dropped the needle-nose pliers into a bin with several other small tools.

"Any of them look familiar?" Linc set a thick notebook with laminated pages back on the shelf.

"Tools? Most of these I've used at one time or another. It comes in handy to be able to fix carts, shelves, and my own bicycle." She sent him a smile in the shaded tool shed. "Now this ..." She drew a long pry bar from the shelf and held it by the curved portion. "I've never used one this large. A short person like me could use it as a cane." She took a pair of small steps. "After adding a rubber tip. What do you use it for?"

"Moving rocks. And other heavy things." Linc took a gulp of water and skimmed his arm across his chin. "Van's loaded except for us. Let's go beat the storm."

She set the pry bar on a stack of folded tarps and walked outside. Thick clouds, turning from moderate to dangerous gray, rose like yeast dough from the northern horizon. At least, she thought it was north. It could be halfway to west considering the number of turns to her internal compass today. She glanced over in time to watch Linc snap a padlock on the shed latch and spin the combination to a random number. "I'll get the gate."

"Thanks."

A few moments later Mona held her breath as they bumped through the monster pothole near the end of the driveway.

"Remind me to fix this before deep frost." He flashed a grin as he pulled onto the road.

Not if I leave tomorrow. Since lunch she'd been having an internal debate while her stomach went up and down the array of blender speeds. For the moment it had settled at stir, the next to lowest on the scale. In ten minutes, three miles, she'd have another human face to look at, someone to change the topic. "Who's Kathy?"

"Uh ... Daryl's sweetheart." He jabbed a finger toward an approaching vehicle. "Is that—? By God, it is. I've only seen one before, at an auto show."

Mona stared with her mouth open at the red El Camino as it approached, rolled on toward the farm, and crested the hill behind them. *No. How?*

"Hey. You okay? You look pale as my shirt."

"That ..." She collected a mouthful of air and forced it down to her lungs before putting her hands to her cheeks. "Basil. His flashy ... El Camino. He ... must have traced your van from the airport. Can we stop and get my things at your apartment before I vanish?"

"Wait a minute. Basil, the same criminal you're hiding from, is here?"

"Unless ... unless there's two of those cars, or trucks, or crossover things in red running around." She shrank tiny in the seat.

"Not likely." He checked his mirrors. "He didn't turn around. You could hide in plain sight. Among friends."

I don't have enough friends to waste any. "You still intend to stop for supper with Daryl?"

"Still need to eat. Anyway, it's time for a pit stop." He braked to a full stop at the intersection of Front and Elm.

"I'd feel better with more than three miles between me and Basil."

Linc parked the van but made no move to get out. "The way I look at it, he's less likely to attempt anything if you're in a group."

"Short term." She could see Linc's reasoning. Maybe for the next few hours it would work. But sooner or later Basil would get desperate enough and put both her and any companions at risk. "I'll take the first bus in the morning."

Five minutes later, face and hands washed, Mona left the tiny restroom and joined Linc at a corner table. She held her breath as a stranger entered before she selected a chair against the wall. At the first hint of Basil she'd—what? Dash to the ladies' room? Hide behind Linc? Or would she be brave enough to make a scene, expose him as a bully? One thing for certain: she would not go with him willingly.

"I'm going up to the bar to order. What do you want to drink?"

"Beer, if we're eating pizza. Any variety on tap." She forced her lips into a cheerful shape as she scanned the patrons at tables along the windows and sitting at the bar. A man with his back to them leaned over the pool table and the brunette with him laughed. "Surprise me."

"Back in a minute."

She busied her hands with the salt and pepper shakers and kept her gaze on Linc striding across the room. A girl could get used to looking at a man like that. He demonstrated the sort of strength that came from daily physical work, not set exercises in a gym.

"Here we go. Four Leinenkugel Red. Your pizza just went in the oven." A server unloaded her tray as Linc and Daryl and Kathy, who'd been playing pool, crossed the room.

"Mona, meet Kathy. And you remember Daryl from earlier?"

"I'm unforgettable." Daryl moved a chair beside Mona and set his back three-quarters to the pine paneling.

Kathy extended her hand. "Pardon his manners. Too many years in law enforcement make it impossible for him to sit in public without his back against the wall. Literally."

Mona cooperated with the handshake and filed it in memory as confident. She glanced at Daryl and wondered how she'd missed it at the orchard. The dress shirt and black dress pants fit him like a uniform and he'd managed to turn any personal question aside with a few words and a hint of a lopsided smile.

"And you, of course, have no irritating habits." Daryl sipped beer while staring into Kathy's face.

"I'll confess to workaholic. Unless you count keeping company with you." A light manner and trace of a smile implied this was an exchange replayed often.

"She only has two jobs." Linc addressed Mona. "To clarify, you're dining with a nurse administrator and mayor. Plus Daryl and me."

Tension drained out through Mona's toes. The nurses, as opposed to a majority of the doctors, had treated her and Matt with respect and genuine concern during the worst twelve days of her life.

"You're early. Didn't expect you for another fifteen minutes or so." Daryl didn't let the silence stretch.

"That storm you mentioned is building. I didn't care to get wet." A gust of wind strong enough to rattle the window behind Linc and a rumble of thunder underlined his words.

"Hazard of living in the valley. Not much sky to forecast from."

"Mayor?" Mona traced her finger down the length of her glass and recalled her only other encounter with a mayor. One year she'd worked as part of a catering crew and the mayor of Minneapolis attended as the featured speaker at a holiday banquet. What did one say? "I shopped at Harter's this morning. Nice place."

"Yes, it is. We've got a good mix of businesses in town." Kathy displayed her fingers. "Beauty shop added a part-time manicurist last year. Bookstore across the street opened a few months ago. Our newest addition."

Mona stared in amazement.

"We're a small place." Kathy turned her smile into a light laugh. "You'll find that everyone knows their neighbor's business. Or thinks they do."

The server returned carrying a large, fragrant pizza with mozzarella still bubbling. "More to drink?"

"Not yet." Daryl saluted her with his almost-full glass.

Mona teased a wedge of pizza onto a small plate.

Linc asked a question of local interest and soon everyone except Mona was discussing the recent Memorial Day ceremonies.

She followed the conversation the best she could without being able to attach faces to any of the names. Each time the door opened she sent her gaze over Kathy's shoulder. Dread yielded to relief when each customer failed to be Basil.

"No more beer for me. I'd have to let Mona drive us home." Linc shook his head when the server returned.

Kathy popped the final bit of crust into her mouth. "So?"

"I don't drive," Mona replied.

"At all?"

"I've never even started a car." She leaned back in her chair, aware it was impossible to escape Daryl's frequent inspection but determined to not let her concern show. Matt had learned to drive. Most of her friends kept valid licenses. Her best friend, Jennifer, owned a car.

"We'll have to cure that." Linc sent her half a smile. "Next time we visit the orchard, maybe tomorrow, I'll start you off on the tractor."

"You might be wasting your time." *I could be hundreds of miles away.*

He shrugged. "Mother keeps telling me to develop patience. Teaching you might be good for both of us."

"We'll see." She tucked her napkin under the edge of her empty plate.

Daryl slid a business card, face down, toward Mona. "Any time you need to talk."

She covered it with one hand and glanced at Linc before speaking. "Any topic?"

"Did he ask you?"

Heat flashed across her face and she became grateful for the subdued tavern lighting. Regardless of the sort of law enforcement this man represented, she wanted to keep a good impression with Linc's friend. "I'm thinking about it."

"Don't think too long." He gestured for the server's attention.

"Ready to go?" Linc rested one hand on top of hers.

Every nerve from the wrist down stirred, urging her to rotate her hand and lace fingers with him. No, it would be foolish and premature, and would steer conversation between here and Eau Claire in exactly the wrong direction. He was a decent man, too good to expose to the cape of trouble attached to her shoulders.

* * *

Basil parked on the far side of Daniel's truck to minimize notice from the road. He stood beside his El Camino for a long moment, thinking of the white van he'd met less than two miles back. Could that be the one Mona rode away in? He'd been distracted by the voice of the GPS and didn't read enough of the license plate to be certain. The van he sought wasn't parked on the village streets this afternoon. He'd checked carefully while making two passes on both main streets. He'd make another circuit around town after his business here. Maybe the place livened up a bit on a Saturday night.

He checked once more that his phone remained clipped to his belt, glanced at the dark clouds rolling in, and walked up the ramp to the sliding door open the width of a man.

A low groan wafted up from the barn's lower level. Basil tensed, waited for his eyes to adjust to the shadowed depths of the hay storage area, and started down steep, wooden steps.

Metal laboratory stands, broken glassware, and light aluminum trays lay scattered and smashed around the large wooden work table. A yellow liquid dripped from a broken beaker to the cement floor. One of three hot plates rested on its side against a fallen wooden stool. The previous laboratory of clean, orderly equipment heating, distilling, and mixing drug ingredients notable on his previous visit appeared to have suffered a tornado. Or an explosion. He glanced at the stout wood beams overhead and noticed lack of charring, or even scorch marks.

"Help … here."

Basil turned his head toward the sound. A moment later he moved toward the weak voice and kicked a shallow pan away from Daniel's foot. His chemist lay on the floor, both legs at unnatural angles and blood seeping through his jeans. One side of his face was swelling to hide an eye and thin lines of red from his nose and mouth merged like streams on a map. Who got here first?

Daniel lifted an arm an inch off his chest and let it drop. "Help me."

"Why?" Basil stepped past him and looked out the window. A lone figure hurried away through the first of the rain. Basil watched the man move along the fence, staying on the narrow strip of grass edging the planted field. "Friend of yours?"

"Call ... nine ... one one."

"Don't think so." Basil squatted outside of Daniel's reach. "Who was here? How many dealers are you cheating?"

"No ... no drugs with ..." Daniel lapsed into silence, exhausted.

"No reason for me to believe you." Basil spied a speckled notebook at the edge of a clear puddle and picked it up with a bandanna from his pocket. "What will I find in here, Daniel? You got the real numbers recorded? What percentage did you claim as 'exclusive'?"

"I ... I ... didn't ... Help ..."

"Exclusive, Daniel." He kicked him in the hip and frowned disgust at the condition of his chemist and the odor of burnt cornstarch and sugar base. "Total. One hundred percent. Every color." He shifted and landed the next kick against the chemist's ribs. "Every last tablet and capsule you mix with MDMA. It all comes to me."

Daniel's cough came out mixed with a choke and another surge of blood at his lips. "Meeer ... cy."

"You don't even beg well." Basil set the book on the table and carefully turned a few pages. He skimmed through notations of cooking times and weights of various ingredients. When he turned the next page he found a narrative. "Who's Linc?"

Daniel's visible eye drifted closed and his groan faded. He rolled his head a few degrees and the intermittent blood droplets emerging from his ear came closer together until they melded into a constant stream.

"Did he beat you?"

"Ahh …"

"Linc's damn trees." Basil read from a diary entry with today's date and tossed more words at Daniel. "How much land do you intend to buy? I haven't paid you enough for more than a few acres. Who else you selling to?"

Basil stared as Daniel's chest rose less and less with each breath. The chemist slipped beyond more than a weak groan as his fingers developed a blue tinge at the tips.

Basil skimmed over several earlier journal entries and smiled as dots of information resolved into a sketch of Linc and Daniel's antagonistic history. He strolled to the door at the end of the barn and discovered it unlatched from the hasty departure of Daniel's assailant. He pushed it open and studied rain soaking into dirt with spaced tufts of grass. The orchard on the far side of a field entrance appeared tidy behind woven wire fence and a steel gate.

What's the quick, easy way to point the authorities to the orchard owner and hide my visit? He returned to take a pair of latex gloves from a box on the floor and kicked Daniel once more to ensure recovery was impossible. For the next few minutes he unmolded and collected every tablet and capsule of E and Molly he could find. He packed the drugs and notebook into a plastic garbage bag and exited via the lower level door.

Enough profit in this bag to keep Kevin in a top-notch rehab facility for a year. He shaped the bag to hide low behind the passenger seat. Then he walked in the thundershower to the orchard gate.

When Basil returned from the tool shed across the lane he carried a tarp and a long, narrow pry bar. He paid careful attention to each footstep and avoided all of the visible liquids and boot prints on the floor. He dropped the heavy tool at the end of the table with a clatter. Finally he squatted beside a silent Daniel, checked for a pulse in the neck, and smiled.

Chapter Eight

Linc rinsed the final specks of shaving cream from his face and reached for the towel. Soft footsteps overhead and the scent of coffee leaking down the stairs confirmed that Mona was still there. Let me protect you. He flipped off the light switch and hurried upstairs. Either he'd be driving her to the Greyhound stop or taking her with him to the orchard. He may as well find out now.

"Morning." Mona lowered two slices of bread in the toaster a moment after he walked into view.

"No 'good' in front of that?" He failed to keep a smile off his face. Her presence in his kitchen, dressed in jeans and tank top, black hair pulled into a ponytail secured with a wide red band, warmed the room better than sunshine.

"You ask for a lot."

He filled the mug sitting next to the coffeemaker and took a cautious sip. "Maybe." He watched her over the rim of his cup and tried to imagine the last few days from her perspective. It was overwhelming. "Do I owe you an apology? An explanation?"

She worked in silence, punctuating her actions with sips of coffee. When a short stack of buttered toast filled two small plates she brought them to the table. "I'm not comfortable with this."

"Which part?" He poured honey-touched oat rounds into a bowl and failed to make eye contact with her. "The marriage proposal? Basil finding Crystal Springs? Or does the idea of Daryl running a background check upset you?"

"Basil. Mostly." She topped off her coffee mug. "You could have mentioned the background check before we were halfway home. When Daryl stopped in at the orchard, for instance."

"I'll put that in the apology column." He added milk to his bowl. "You could call the police." He suggested the same action he'd failed to talk her into during the return to Eau Claire and an hour of conversation in this same room last evening. "He did break into your apartment."

"Yes, he did. Three days ago." She picked up a half slice of toast and set it down again. "Police want proof. Evidence. For all I know Basil's gone back and wiped away any traces he ever entered my place."

"Maybe he didn't recognize my van. Are you sure he took photos?"

"Impossible to prove. It's just ... well ... he has a reputation to maintain. Collecting his due. If he's convinced Matt is hiding money with me, he won't stop."

"Does he carry a gun?"

"Is that where your 'let me protect you' mantra ends?" She bit into her breakfast.

"No."

"He has a history of using his fists. Or, in Matt's case, hiring others."

Linc studied her face and fought the urge to reach across the table. His fingers yearned to caress her deepening worry lines away. "Two against him sounds better than one."

"No police. I won't put Matt's blood on my hands." She pushed back her chair. "We should get going. I've a row of trees to finish."

*　*　*

Mona filled the long silences during the drive to Crystal Springs with several rounds of examining and discarding her options. They each wore different shapes, the negative points pushing forward for attention ahead of their positive companions. Her breakfast—one slice of toast—poked at her stomach as if it had reassembled and turned to stone.

Her first instinct, delayed after Linc's presentation of confidence in his ability to protect her, remained flight. Milwaukee beckoned. It was large enough to hide in a crowd. She could blend in, find a job off the books either cooking or cleaning. Within a few days a pre-paid phone and post office box would enable contact with Matt. And give Basil's inside men a trail of breadcrumbs.

Did drug kingpins have inter-city networks? She shivered under another of Linc's large, long-sleeved shirts on loan.

Linc's marriage proposal tempted her like a cinnamon roll drizzled with a butter and pecan glaze. Then the caution flag popped into view. Marriage was serious, a promise to God as well as the other person. This one, if she agreed at all, needed conditions. Limits. Protection and a respectable status tempted her. Would he restrict or smother her progress toward the restaurant dream? Marriage gave him land. She gained—? She glanced at his face in profile as he drove. Companionship? A friend? Was that enough?

"Deep thoughts?" Linc turned at the Front Street entrance to the village.

"Private. Making a decision." She skipped a heartbeat as an ambulance approached, no lights flashing and siren quiet. She turned and read River County Ambulance District #3 on the side of the boxy vehicle. She kept her gaze focused on it until it turned west on the federal highway and drove out of sight. The incident cooled her skin like an out-of-place breeze. "Is that unusual?"

"To see an ambulance?"

"It didn't seem to be in much of a hurry." She called up several instances when she'd cycled out of traffic at the sound and sight of emergency vehicles.

"Could be a transfer. Or headed back to their base."

"Of course." Logic. She controlled her tongue when it wanted to object to his best-case scenario explanation.

Five minutes later Linc turned into the farm driveway and stopped short.

"What?" They spoke in unison and looked at each other.

Mona gazed out the windshield and began to count police vehicles. Four, five— no, six. A final one blocked the narrow service lane beside the orchard. She opened her mouth to tell Linc to leave but no sound came out.

He eased the van forward, pulled to the edge of the lawn, and let another sheriff's department sedan enter the yard. Two officers emerged from the open barn door before Mona could get a count on the law enforcement personnel moving around the place. One of them pointed to the van as if giving directions. She rubbed her arms, searching for warmth. The last time she'd talked with police her information had confirmed Matt's opportunity to steal. Is it too late to leave?

"Follow my lead." Linc opened his door and stepped to the ground.

Do I have a choice? A moment later she stood at the front bumper of the van, Linc within arm's reach. If she'd been able to raise an arm.

"What happened, officer?"

"A crime."

Mona read "Kingman" on his name tag before he turned his attention from Linc to her. She stared back, silent and determined to stay unnoticed, until he shifted his gaze back to Linc.

"State your name and business here this morning."

"Lincoln Dray. I came to work in my orchard."

The deputy's expression shifted from casual to intense interest. He signaled to another officer with his left hand. The slice of concrete in her stomach shifted, pressed against her ribs. He didn't do anything.

"Sheriff, meet Mr. Dray." Deputy Kingman spoke to a trim woman with insignia on her collar. "And?"

"Mona. Mona Smith." Her strained voice sounded foreign to her ears. She fought the urge to stand at attention under the mere gaze of the woman.

"We have questions." The sheriff pointed to her deputy and then Mona.

"Come with me, Miss ... Smith." The officer consulted his notes while wrapping his words in doubt. He halted just out of comfortable earshot of Linc and the sheriff.

Yes, the name is Smith. Do I need to spell it for you?

"What's your relationship with Mr. Dray?"

He wasn't going to waste time with pleasantries. Good. Shorter would be better. They would leave and she'd be on a bus before dark. "Friend."

"Do you know Daniel Larson?"

"I've heard the name."

"And?"

Mona crossed her arms and raised her chin another degree. What sort of mischief was the owner of the flashy truck parked a dozen yards away involved with? "I've never met him. Linc told me he rents the farmhouse."

"Have you been on this farm before today?"

"Once." Silence filled the gap between her and the officer, stretched to uncomfortable, and she broke it. "Yesterday." She allowed silence to grow again until he shifted weight from one foot to the other, his pen poised above paper. "He sprayed trees. I trimmed grass."

"And you didn't speak with Mr. Larson?"

"No." She continued with short responses, making the officer work for the information. Several questions covered their arrival and departure times until she ran out of ways to reply that she'd not checked her watch at every pause in her work. The officer gathered the approximate time Daniel's truck arrived, and the position of the barn door when they drove away. Then he reviewed what appeared to be a list of each building, shed, and shelter on the farm, asking if she'd entered them.

He turned to a fresh page in his notebook. "Almost done. I just need to see your identification. And we need to get your prints."

She moved her gaze from his hands to his eyes and stayed silent.

"For elimination."

Without a word she pulled her State of Minnesota non-driver card out of her back jeans pocket and extended it in two fingers.

"Is this your current address?"

"My mail's delivered there." She stayed on the knife edge of truth. The odds of returning to the apartment, even to retrieve mail, dropped below those of a lightning bolt appearing in the cloudless morning sky.

Two long minutes later, Deputy Kingman escorted her to the Crime Scene Unit van. He called out to one of the technicians that she needed to be fingerprinted.

"What sort of crime are you investigating?" she asked, a variation of Linc's initial question.

"Murder. Daniel Larson is dead. His grandfather found him this morning, wrapped in a tarp like a giant egg roll in front of the orchard shed."

Dead? Here? She shoved her hands deep into her jeans pockets to hide their shaking. Something happened after they left the orchard yesterday. And she couldn't stop her mind from drawing a direct line from the dead renter to Basil. She swallowed hard and prayed the River County Sheriff found evidence to solve this without another word from either her or Linc.

"Right hand, please."

Mona cooperated as the evidence technician rolled her fingers over the electronic pad. She glanced back to the van in time to see Linc and the sheriff approach.

"Print Mr. Dray next. He's consented to boot prints and a field search of the van." Sheriff Bergstrom inspected Mona for a long moment.

Boots? Mona couldn't see anything unusual about the dark brown work boots on Linc's feet. Did the police have tracks they wanted to compare?

"Yes, ma'am. Almost done with Ms. Smith." The young lady rolled Mona's left pinkie and released her hand. A moment later she returned Mona's ID from the clip attached to the computerized fingerprint module.

Mona moistened her lips and hesitated beside Linc. "What next?"

"Follow directions. Leave the portable circus." He waved one hand to indicate the controlled chaos of the farmyard.

Chapter Nine

"I know what I saw, Mr. Frieberg." Mona rested her palms on the counter of the small outer office of Frieberg Investigations. For the past half hour she, Linc, and Daryl had talked in a circle about her flight from Minneapolis and the sighting of the El Camino yesterday.

"I still think if he recognized the van he would have returned to town and been waiting for us outside Jack's." Linc looked straight at her. "We don't know where he was going. Hilltop isn't the only farm on that road."

"What other business would a man like Basil have in Crystal Springs?"

Linc shoved both hands in his jeans pockets. "What about it, Daryl? Daniel boasted he would buy the farm by the end of summer. I don't see how he'd have the money. It makes me think he was doing something illegal in the barn."

Daryl tapped his pen at the bottom of his notes. "The sheriff needs time and space to work. The village grapevine has been quiet about Daniel. That doesn't rule out illegal activity, but it does imply he didn't deal local. If—and I stress the word 'if'—Basil went to Hilltop, he would leave a trace. Everyone does."

"It rained," Mona reminded them.

"Any tire tracks are lost in all the police vehicles by now. They may have been washed out before Old Joe Larson found his grandson." Linc gazed out to Front Street. "I didn't like the tone of some of the questions. At least a few of the deputies have me in the guilty column."

"They need evidence." Daryl pushed away from the counter.

"We were together. I'm your alibi for the afternoon." Mona rubbed her arms to counter a sudden chill. Police made her nervous. She'd witnessed one of Matt's arrests and that was too many.

"Yes," Linc agreed. "And I couldn't ask for a better or more beautiful one. Truth wins in the end, right?"

"You two go on. Do whatever young people do on a Sunday." Daryl closed the folder in front of him.

Mona sat still, aware the investigator's blue eyes missed nothing.

"Don't run." Daryl's voice drifted across the counter. "Stay with Lincoln, return to your Minneapolis apartment, or call me. Anything else will paint you guilty."

Did this man read people as easily as others skimmed magazines? Or had she lost the ability to hide her intentions? "Since you phrase it like that."

"I'll open a line of communication with the sheriff."

A quarter hour later, Mona glanced in the side mirror for the third time in as many miles. "Are we being followed?"

"Maybe." Linc slowed and took the truck lane up the next hill.

Please, no. She grasped her seat belt and turned to look out the undersized windows in the rear doors. A small red sedan continued behind them, ignoring the easy opportunity to pass. "In the movies we'd manage to lose him."

"I left my stunt driver hat back in the college dorm. How do you feel about stopping for lunch?"

"I'm not hungry." The slab of concrete called breakfast remained whole, merely softened around the edges during the past hour. Any addition would be unwelcome in her stomach.

"I hear a Coke calling my name." He accelerated to the speed limit and held steady until they reached the city limits of the largest town on their route.

"Hope you have an internal compass." Five minutes and six turns on residential streets later, Mona sighted a familiar fast food sign ahead. The red car followed like a trained dog on an invisible leash.

"Confirming our suspicions. Is this your criminal acquaintance?"

"I've only paid attention to his flashy car."

"For my peace of mind, grab my phone from the console. And don't hesitate to dial the cops if it is Basil and he pulls something, like ramming us."

She lapsed into silence as Linc ordered them each a pop in the drive-thru and pulled ahead to the service window. Their tail parked on the edge of the lot. How many different rides did Basil have access to? Matt estimated the organization at well over two dozen dealers and thieves. If even a third of them owned vehicles, Basil could demand use of a variety. "What do we do next?"

"Drive to Eau Claire." Linc jabbed a straw into his drink and parked it in the cup holder.

"So he knows where you live?"

"I didn't say anything about driving to the house."

"No police." Mona sipped Sprite and reviewed her interview with Deputy Kingman. She'd followed her own advice of answering every question but volunteering nothing. The officer hadn't asked much of her history. And while he'd posed three questions concerning the time they'd left the farm and arrived at Jack's on Saturday, he hadn't questioned her as to number, makes, or models of vehicles encountered on the trip to town. She tapped her fingertips against the side of her plastic cup and imagined what the official background check would find.

Daryl described his findings on her as "clean" when asked today. Another farmhouse came in and out of view at the end of a curved drive. Would Matt's conviction spill over and point police in the wrong direction?

"Think about a shopping list. It's ten miles to the store."

"We're buying groceries?" She studied Linc's profile.

"My cook mentioned a lack of produce. It's a public place. On a Sunday afternoon it should be busy enough to raise a problem or two for our uninvited companion."

"We still need to go home. Eventually." Basil wasn't the sort of person to give up just because they detoured to a supermarket.

"Before the ice cream melts and the milk goes sour."

She surprised herself with a smile. "Guess I know what's at the top of your shopping list. What else?"

"Supper. Do you think you'll be able to make and eat a super-sized salad?"

"Affirmative on the first part." Her drink melted more of that hard lump in her stomach but it still strayed far from normal. A vanishing act by the car trailing them was the best medicine she could think of.

"Good. We'll stick to basics for the rest. I favor sandwiches for brown bag lunches and quick prep for the other meals. Do you have a problem with that?"

"No." Selecting the groceries loomed as another area for uncomfortable questions. Should she encourage him to buy items she enjoyed cooking? Or tell him to ignore her and buy only for one? Staying at his place if she declined his marriage proposal would be cruel. Then again, she'd neither finalized nor presented her conditions to accept. The entire question had slipped down in priority the instant police cars on the farm came into view.

Ten minutes later Mona walked beside Linc toward the main entrance of a large, colorful supermarket sign. "We should start with salad greens."

He claimed a cart and headed toward a display of local strawberries and California grapes. While he selected from the daily specials, she tucked three varieties of leaf lettuce into plastic bags and stashed them in the cart's child seat.

"Radishes." He pointed.

Yes, sir. She nodded silent approval as he bagged a small purple cabbage. When the basics for grand salads rested in the cart they moved around the corner to the dairy department and a dozen aisles of boxed, canned, and frozen foods.

"Frozen juice." He appeared to consult a mental checklist. "Oh, did you use the last jar of spaghetti sauce Friday?"

"I didn't see another. Do you want the same kind again?" She waited for his nod before backtracking two aisles to pasta, sauces, and box dinners.

She glanced in both directions before turning to face the display of jars. One customer shopped at the other end of the row. Sunday afternoon didn't appear to be a popular time for shopping in the central aisles.

"Mona Smith." Strong fingers wrapped around her upper arm as the deep, harsh voice spoke her name.

She jerked back half a step and opened her mouth to scream. Basil's hand pressed across her lips, muffling her voice to a murmur. Her hands opened and the jar of roasted garlic chunky tomato sauce crashed and splattered at her feet.

"Not a word. Got it?"

She nodded. She breathed deeply and pulled cigar scent from his skin with a few of her scattered senses.

"Who is he?" He relaxed the grip on her arm without letting go.

Mona darted her gaze over his shoulder, behind her, everywhere except his face.

"What's Dray to you?"

"A friend." She stared at him for the first time after the instant of recognition. How did he know Linc's name? What else did he know?

"Did you give him the money?"

"I ... I ... don't have money." She swallowed down a portion of fear mixed with a plea for Matt's safety. "I never did. You ... got bad info."

"Is that what your brother claims?" He squeezed her upper arm tight enough to leave a bruise.

She opened her mouth and closed it without a sound. Matt didn't give her details of his freelance work. She clenched her free hand as she realized the source of the most recent hospital bill credit. Matt had given her money. In his own mixed-up version of morality, he'd used illegal cash to reduce the family debt.

"How much?" Basil lowered his voice but invaded her space.

"Less than five grand. He spent it before his arrest." She found a bit of courage and looked him in the face. "He claimed it was a freelance job. Same as the night he got arrested with a few hundred on him. You heard all about that incident." Sweat trickled and stalled at the neckline of her tank top.

"Then give me information. Recent, since your precious brother was sentenced."

"I don't have any of that either."

He curled his lips into a fake smile. "Don't be so sure."

"I'll scream for the police before I deal drugs or steal for you." She blinked and tried to banish the rumors that women around Basil had a habit of getting arrested. One convicted felon in the family was more than enough.

"Comments like that put ideas into a man's head. I want silence." He released her arm. "The last time you saw me was at the airport."

"But ... your car ... El—"

"Not since Thursday afternoon. Got it?"

"Don't hurt Matt."

"You and Mr. Dray stay deaf, dumb, and blind to a certain incident yesterday and Matt's safe as the governor himself. Talk, and ... well, you're bright enough to figure it out."

Silence instead of money. Relief flowed up from her toes and halted. She and Linc had mentioned the El Camino to Daryl in today's conversation. The investigator would not forget.

"Smart girl. We'll talk again." Basil turned and hurried to the end of the aisle and out of sight.

"Hey." Linc's single word startled her.

"Sorry, had a small problem." She snatched another jar of sauce and stepped out of the mess on the floor. "We'd better find an employee for a wet clean-up in aisle seven."

* * *

Mona reached into the pantry with a long wooden spoon. She stretched out her arm, swept the tool a fraction of an inch above the shelf, and felt it make contact with something in the shadows.

A moment later she prodded a box of chocolate pudding mix toward the edge. She tipped the container, checking for leaks and searching for the sell-by date. As the first grains of finely powdered milk and cocoa sifted out, she tossed it to the garbage can. She leaned forward again, guiding the spoon along the edge all the way to the back, checking for stray objects. Every square inch of kitchen counter and half of the floor lay covered with cans, boxes, and plastic storage containers from the deep pantry shelves.

As soon as the perishable groceries were stored, she'd begun this project. If her hands stayed busy, maybe her mind could take a break.

Basil wants silence. It sounded simple compared to a demand for nonexistent money. But the silence he requested wasn't hers to grant. Daryl knew from today's meeting in his office that the red El Camino they'd met on the road belonged to a drug kingpin and it was headed toward Hilltop.

Not telling Linc of the encounter and request in aisle seven today beckoned as the most sensible idea. She didn't have the energy at the moment to defend her position against reporting the incident to the police. It wasn't as if they could arrest the man for following them. She'd find a time to tell him. He tended to be relaxed and most talkative in the evening, over what he called his ritual dish of ice cream before bed.

Linc wants a wife. She leaned into the pantry and coaxed a can of kidney beans forward. A legal marriage would tie her to Eau Claire—and Crystal Springs. The option of taking the bus to a new place had vanished during the interview on the farm. She couldn't return to Minneapolis either. A lump of stubbornness lodged in her throat. She longed for freedom of movement, at least the illusion of control over her life.

Did she want to stay? Live with Linc? Spend every night listening for stray sounds from his side of the wall and—and what? She couldn't find a word. Expecting? Dreading? Wanting a soft rap on her door?

She checked the condition of the can in her hand, found the date, and added it to the section of items to keep. Rules. This sudden marriage needs rules. Her skin rippled with the memory of Linc's hand over hers at the orchard, at supper, unloading groceries. She looked at the closed office door and listened to a printer click as if starting a new assignment. Separate bedrooms floated to the top of her mental list of marriage conditions.

Once more she bent between the two lower shelves, guided the wooden spoon along the far edge and curled it forward. A loose wad of paper rolled ahead of it.

She picked up the paper by an exposed edge and moved her hand toward the trash.

"Hey." Linc stepped out of the office.

Mona's hand waved the paper and it began to uncrumple. A fancy golden letterhead came into view. She gave it one firm shake while tightening her hold on the corner. "What's this?"

"Looks like a letter. Where did you ..." He gave a low whistle as he gazed over the pantry contents taking over the kitchen. "I thought you were doing a load of laundry."

"I was. I am. Multitasking."

"Impressive."

She sat down on a wooden chair pulled away from the dining table and smoothed the letter. Three lawyer names and the logo of the Wisconsin State Bar Association greeted her above a single-spaced huge paragraph. A large signature in purple ink decorated the bottom. "It's from your knife-holding friend Tami."

"Ex. Ex-girlfriend. Ex-fiancée." Color matching the label on tomato paste advanced up his neck, gaining inches between each word.

Mona narrowed her gaze to focus on certain phrases. "She calls you a draconian slave driver."

"She was angry when she wrote that." He stepped beside her and made one attempt to pull the paper away. "I thought I threw it away. That's where it belongs."

"Finder." Mona jerked the letter out of his reach and scanned further into the mass of words. "Chauvinistic Neanderthal." She raised her gaze to his face. Which was the true Linc? The oppressive monster of this letter? Or the positive actions of work ethic and kindness of the last few days? "Tami seems to have a good vocabulary. Lawyer?"

"Paralegal. She used letterhead from her father's firm."

"Leech draining the lifeblood from others before spitting them out." Mona picked another of Tami's phrases. "How long did you know each other?"

"She exaggerates. Two years ... maybe a month over that. Why?"

"Hmmm." Mona folded the letter into quarters and tucked it into the waistband of her running shorts. Later, away from his direct influence, she'd read the entire rant and do her own sorting of truth from fiction. At the moment a slender thread connected her to the woman. She wanted a little time and space to get acquainted with a girl who would abandon Linc a few weeks before their wedding. She looked at him and realized he'd hardly let her out of his sight since Friday. Did he intend to keep her on an invisible leash?

"Do you want help getting this put away again?" He picked up a can and frowned at the label. "I don't remember buying half of this."

"Do the shelves come out? Do you have paper for fresh liners?"

"Good questions." He squatted down to examine the bottom of the lowest shelf. A moment later he popped it up, angled it out, and extended it toward her. "You're taking this cook and housekeeper position seriously."

"I'm a thoughtful person." She propped the plywood square in front of the dishwasher and prepared to grab the next one.

"Tami." He tapped the next shelf free. "She didn't want to live on the farm. Call me stupid or infatuated or blind, your choice. I ignored the signs while Grandmother was alive. I missed other things too."

"Like …"

"She hesitated to set a wedding date. Flirted with my friends. My brother. And his friends."

She waited while he changed position and pushed up on the final shelf. In the three days of their acquaintance she was getting used to conversations filled with silent spaces from tiny to elongated.

"Then Adam moved back in with his parents after college. December. Mid-year graduate. He made a full-time job out of an employment search. Tami skipped flirting and went directly for the software engineer's vital parts."

"He got a job in California." Mona tested her memory of his sparse comments in the orchard.

Linc nodded. "Mr. Dense and Trusting ... me ... finally wised up and confronted her on January twenty-second. It didn't go well." He rubbed the scar on his arm. "While I spent hours in emergency getting stitched back together she packed her things and moved in with Adam. I found that ... letter ... the next day. At least she was decent enough to return her keys."

"But—"

"I changed the locks anyway."

"And never thought about her again?" Mona dropped a sponge into a pan of warm water.

"Not exactly." He appeared surprised by his own laugh. "I found occasion to curse her regularly for weeks. Now it's irregular."

"Recovering from a wounded heart?"

"From this distance it's more like crushed pride. I'll go look for new paper. Once upon a time I had a roll in the downstairs storage cubby." And with that, he was gone.

* * * *

Mona paused in the doorway between foyer and garage. The large door stood wide open, allowing early evening light and the scent of hot charcoal from down the street to enter. She glanced around for Linc. Was he outside? Talking to a neighbor? She closed the small door and walked along the side of the van.

"Hey. You found me. You're just in time to supervise." Linc squatted by an open can of red-brown stain and stirred it with a wooden paddle.

"We need to talk." The confidence she'd gathered together while cleaning up the kitchen began to seep out of her toes as she watched his hands. Every micro-movement as he removed the stirrer and set it aside on the lid invited her to touch him. Bad idea. She tucked her hands behind her back and tried for a casual pose.

"Go ahead. I can listen and stain these planters at the same time."

"You'll need to do some talking too." She waited for his nod. "At the store today. Basil found me."

His brush stroke wavered on raw wood. "And you didn't say anything until now?" He turned to face her, his brush forgotten and dripping stain on a tarp. "Four, five hours later?"

"He knows your name. I don't know how. But he called you Dray." She identified anger as it crossed his eyes and waited until it was replaced by the more frequent cool determination. "He's not after money. We ... Basil and I ... got straight on that."

"What does he want? He didn't follow us for most of an hour and seek you out without a reason."

"Silence. He wants both of us to keep quiet." She pressed her lips tight for an instant to let her tongue and brain get coordinated. "He wants me to say the last time I saw him was at the airport. We're to claim we haven't seen him or his El Camino since then."

"It's too late for that. Or did you forget about our conversation with Daryl?"

"I remember it well." If she closed her eyes for a moment she could picture the retired Secret Service agent now. He had looked at her with outward casual interest while clearly seeing every little movement and hearing every inflection in her voice.

"And when Basil finds out?"

"He'll have to find me first."

"Run and hide. Is that your answer to problems?"

"No." Mona shifted her weight but didn't retreat as he stood and passed her with long strides. Tami's negative words from the letter she'd managed to read twice rose in her throat. No, she'd not resort to copying another person's insults.

He jerked open the van passenger door and reached for the glove box. "Does Basil steal cars?"

"Probably. In the past. I think he orders others now." She exhaled a bit of her tension. He'd not touched her. He showed more control than a lot of men.

"Explains how he got my name. Ninety-nine percent certain he took the address too." He held up the van registration papers.

"We couldn't have been the only people to notice his El Camino yesterday. It doesn't blend in."

"And that may be the only thing preventing another visit from your non-friend. Why didn't you call the police? Or let me call them ... before this?"

"Matt." She marched forward until her toes were within an inch of Linc's worn sneakers, releasing a bubble of defensive anger in each step. "Basil's minions in prison already beat my brother once. Told him it was initiation. I don't want my brother to die. Is that wrong?"

"Okay, okay. Don't go all martial arts on me." Linc opened his arms and dropped them to his sides.

She stared into his face long and hard. Any person with brain function should understand she wouldn't tolerate him stepping between her and Matt. She didn't want to calculate the diminishing effect caused by their difference in height.

A full minute later, Linc sighed and took one step back. "I think it's time you told me exactly how your brother ended up in prison."

"Agreed." She leaned against the van and concentrated on keeping her skin of strength visible. This wasn't the conversation she'd intended for this evening but if she watched his reactions closely she should get a clue as to how much of Tami's letter was exaggeration in the heat of the moment.

She waited for him to toss the papers into the glove box and return to the staining project before she took a seat on an overturned pail. "It's neither complicated nor unusual. Matt picked some wrong friends in junior high and they started with petty theft. He didn't stop when he was caught."

Tomorrow at lunch. As she talked about her brother and fielded questions and comments from Linc, the deadline for a decision on the marriage proposal grew like an evening shadow.

Chapter Ten

Linc checked the time twice after completing his interior garden work at the insurance office. Either his personal state of mind or the unsettled weather charged the space around him, but each client this morning had managed to find something to complain about. Mondays already boasted a negative reputation; at this rate he'd be alone and dining on a frozen dinner tonight.

He sighed and mixed it with a silent prayer for at least one thing to go well today. His call to the River County Sheriff's Department beeped and whirred next to his ear. "This is Lincoln Dray. Can you tell me if the crime scene at five twenty-three County T has been released?"

"One moment, please."

He tapped one thumb against the steering wheel in tempo to the generic piano music on his phone.

"Mr. Dray?"

"Yes, I'm here." He breathed a small sigh of relief. It was the same male voice; perhaps Linc could repeat his question one less time.

"Only a portion of that scene has been processed."

"I'm interested in the orchard. And the tool shed within those fenced acres."

Portions of mumbled words replaced music for long moments. "Do you have domestic animals in the enclosure?"

"No, sir. Only things within the fence are apple trees, grass, and the equipment to care for them. No stock." He frowned at the dashboard. Any law enforcement official in a rural county would have written livestock into their report. With a dozen or more officers and all the activity yesterday, domestic animals and deputies would have come face to face. He tried during the next silence to imagine a few calves contaminating a crime scene and prancing out the gate to sniff all the vehicles and humans.

"Good. One moment, please."

Linc opened his mouth to ask for a simple yes or no and closed it without a sound. Making any sort of irritating remark needed to stay at the bottom of his priorities with the sheriff's department. He didn't want to move up on the suspect list. They had enough to do. How many murders in River County? One every five years? Less?

"Sir?" A new voice, female and authoritative, came on the line.

"Yes, ma'am."

"The crime scene remains under active investigation."

Linc swallowed. This sounded like Sheriff Bergstrom, the same person who'd questioned him carefully yesterday. "All of it? I'd really like to have access to the orchard and tool shed. I have no interest in going into the barn or house."

"Check back in twenty-four hours, Mr. Dray. Your trees aren't going to wither away before then."

"Yes, ma'am. I'll call again tomorrow. Thank you for your time."

Ten minutes later, Linc parked in front of the Polk Street house where Mona was working today. Casual comments from Lorraine Terrier at the greenhouse this morning had indicated enough work remained for the entire week. Maybe. No, don't get your hopes up. He hunted for confidence. If he walked in to face Mona over lunch with a defeated attitude she'd be right to refuse marriage and demand a ride to the bus station.

I'll miss her. He found it more difficult each day to keep his hands off. Yesterday, it had taken all the self-control he could find when he'd glimpsed her fine tush covered by purple running shorts while her head and shoulders poked into the pantry. She stood on a fine set of legs. And she had eyes that he wanted to gaze into to discover the secrets of the galaxy.

Wise up. She said all of three words over breakfast today. Not a good sign.

"Hey." He announced his entrance inside the utility room door.

"You're late." She said it with a smile and pointed to the sink. "Wash up and I'll put the tuna filling on the buns."

"Looks good." Did he mean the table set for a picnic or the female in the jeans?

"Lorraine went to have lunch with her husband."

"I figured as much when I didn't see her Jeep." He grabbed a towel from a drawer handle. The question of his future rested with her, the petite figure with dark, unique eyes that he wanted to learn to read. His stomach twisted in anticipation of bad news, injuring any appetite remaining after his morning. He braced his hips against the counter and faced her. "Have you made a decision? On the ... marriage?"

"I've been compiling a list. Some items are non-negotiable."

Not a flat-out "no." He listened as his breathing returned toward normal. A moment later he joined her at the table. "We'll start there. If you wish."

"Separate bedrooms." She picked up a pencil and poised it at the first item on an agenda.

He looked away from her face, and failed to find any response to cancel the arrangement he'd included with the initial proposal. Maybe they could hold a private negotiation at a later date. He nodded. "Next."

He agreed without hesitation to several items, including her desire to keep her own name.

"Debt." She moistened her lips with one pass of her tongue. "Everything up to the wedding day stays separate. I ... won't drag your credit down."

"How bad is it?"

"My credit rating? In actual numbers?" She circled one fork tine on her paper plate. "I've never worked up enough courage to check. Do they go into single digits?"

"Are you sure you're not confusing yourself with your brother?" He took a guess that a convicted burglar would rate below a working waitress.

"No matter. Do we keep it separate?"

Linc reached over and placed one finger under her chin. "Look at me. Give me more than a glance." He waited until she complied and gazed into eyes that tempted him with secrets. "I like you, Mona. I enjoy your company. I even understand a point of pride about the medical bills. I doubt I could pay them if I wanted."

"So you agree?"

"For the moment." His thumb stroked her smooth, perfect cheek. "Are you done with the list?"

"The important items." She blinked twice and looked away.

"Will you keep them open to future negotiation?" He didn't care which name she used or which job she worked. He recognized this relationship as out of the ordinary, very sudden, and too fragile to demand a shared bed. In the future? The near future? How many more nights would he survive mentally undressing her before falling into a restless sleep?

"I can do that."

"In that case." He stood, went to her, and tugged her to her feet. Heat poured from her hands, warming his arms until he glanced down to see if they glowed. He fumbled with a mouth as dry as fall leaves for a long moment. "Mary Monica, 'call me Mona,' Smith. Will you marry me?"

She squeezed both of his hands before fixing him with a wide-eyed stare. Muscle by muscle her lips moved into a smile. "Yes."

* * *

Mona gazed into gray eyes that lightened into a smile. My fiancé. What have I done?

"Thank you." The joy swept over his face quicker than a blush. "May I?"

She stood still, processing the verbal exchange, lost in her own answer. Then his lips touched hers, brushed her smile, and lingered.

Comfort. Safety. She closed her eyes and molded her lips against his warm flesh. Perfect fit. "Mmmm."

He released her mouth and she started to object. Then he returned. Firm. Seeking. The tip of his tongue searched along the seam of her mouth, unzipping reluctant muscles.

Her hands skimmed up his arms and continued until they laced on the back of his neck. She breathed in delicate flavors of parsley and celery seed mixed with warm promise. Time stretched, every instant of the kiss, every point of contact between them burrowing into her memory.

"Agreed." He retreated a few inches, breaking the spell.

Mona leaned forward and rested her head against his chest. Rapid, steady throbs matched her runaway heart. She blinked his shoes into focus. "That was ... special."

He nuzzled the top of her head, and pulled her close with arms that circled her waist. "Understatement."

Trust and a smile sent doubt scurrying off to a dark corner. The answer, the one she'd been ready to discard a moment before it passed her lips, coated her mouth with contentment. Desire stirred low in her body and sent a ripple of heat to her fingers caressing the back of his neck. She wanted—needed—more.

He eased away and placed one finger on her orphaned lower lip. "Mona."

She brought her hands to his chest and laid them flat against muscles hidden by too much cloth. What happened? She didn't consider herself a novice at kisses. Since age fifteen she'd dated a dozen or more boys. More often than not she'd enjoyed their kissing and caressing. Or at least she'd thought so. Until a moment ago. Or an hour?

"I ... I ..." Linc covered her right hand with his left. "Work."

A car door slammed, jerking a portion of her mind back to reality. They stood in the middle of a kitchen, in a house she was cleaning, and the estate executer would walk through the door any minute now.

She swallowed, pressed her lips for an instant, and found a trace of his flavor. Reality squeezed into the room. "Yes. Work." Don't let go. "What happens now?"

"Immediately?" He lifted one of her hands with a soft grip and guided it toward his mouth. "I'll make a call this afternoon. I know a man with the credentials to marry us."

"And?" She drew in a deep breath and held it as he licked her index finger.

"Do you have a birth certificate?"

Do that again. A few brain cells paused on logical. She forced her mind to picture the papers scattered on the bed before she'd collected them during her hasty departure. "I think so."

"We'll be at the courthouse when it opens in the morning."

"You're not wasting time."

"Time's important. Wisconsin has a waiting period."

The reminder of his deadline, the entire reason for their marriage, slapped against her face like winter air. This was a business transaction. She had agreed to a mutual living agreement to satisfy the terms of a will. The kiss must be an aberration. She dared not forget her real position in his life: public wife and private—friend. "Of course. You'll have time to spare."

"Two days."

She blinked away surprise at his abrupt, no nonsense statement. "You can count on me. I keep my word."

"And which word would that be?" Lorraine stood in the doorway, arms crossed and a wide smile on her face.

"Would you like to attend a wedding?" Linc lowered her hand without releasing it and turned toward the new arrival. "I'm thinking Sunday evening or Monday morning. It will depend on when my friend Ben is available."

"Congratulations. I enjoy weddings." Lorraine advanced a few steps and pulled Linc and then Mona into brief, warm hugs.

Mona followed Linc to the van a few moments later. Desire for another kiss, to test if her memory fooled her, wrestled with the need for practical matters. "I'll see you at the greenhouse?"

"That's the plan." He turned beside the open door. "I'll call Ben and set a time to talk with him."

"And I'll check for the paperwork when we get back to your place."

He reached out and hooked a ponytail escapee behind her ear. "Thank you."

Her breath stuttered at the gentle gesture. "Drive safe."

Chapter Eleven

Basil checked the time and shoved his phone back into his pocket. He'd been watching the greenhouse entrance from this position for more than an hour now. He rolled his shoulders, walked one circle around the faded red sedan, and raised the binoculars again. The only visible activity this late afternoon consisted of one couple loading half a dozen large pots into their SUV and driving away.

Where was Dray? How late did he work? In a few minutes it would be six, past time for any of the clients he'd gathered as references to close. When his phone vibrated he quickly pulled it out and checked the number. Nick again. "Talk to me."

"We got a problem, boss."

Basil sighed. Both sunshine and rain were problems to Nick. Why Basil planned to put him in charge this week he'd never know. Except that his other employees showed even fewer management skills. "Explain."

"The busboy ... from Hiawatha's Griddle."

"I know the one." Broken nose, a busted rib or two, and a couple of lost minutes courtesy of his fists early Saturday morning had prompted his visit to Daniel.

"His manager took him to one of those urgent care places. And now the police are asking questions."

"You don't know anything. You haven't seen me all day."

"Got it. And, boss—"

"Out with it, Nick. I'm working." He raised the binoculars as a Jeep Cherokee halted in front of the greenhouse.

"Will we be getting more product before Friday night?"

"Make all the usual arrangements." Basil ended the call before Nick could bother him with another question. He had enough reserve supply hidden in his office, including two kilos of Molly capsules direct from Daniel's lab to last more than one week.

A few more days, an arrest of another party—Mr. Lincoln Dray, for example—for Daniel Larson's murder, and he'd gather up Kevin and move. North Dakota was full of new money and fresh residents. He'd find a safe place for his brother and attempt honest work for the first time in his life.

He held the field glasses to his eyes as two women, one of them Mona Smith wearing a baseball cap pulled low, exited the Jeep. They unloaded black plastic bags filled to capacity and carted them inside. Five minutes later, Dray arrived in the van, this time with bright signs attached. Basil alternated watching with pacing as the women came outside and helped unload plants and plastic containers. When Dray slammed the rear door of the van closed, another man, hobbling along in a walker, emerged.

Handshakes all around. Small talk. Basil could imagine the quality of the conversation. How long did it take Midwesterners to say goodbye? These people worked together. Looked each other in the eye daily. What could they have to say?

Basil lagged behind the van, allowed one and for half a mile even two vehicles to come between them during the seven miles to Benson Place. He took the next street, circled around, and confirmed Dray's building as the garage door lowered.

She's landed in a nice neighborhood. He drove off and began thinking about travelling with Kevin. It sure would be helpful to have another set of hands. A woman. Like Mona. He'd make sure she got word of Matt's next beating and then she'd come along, pretend to be a cousin. Or girlfriend. He smiled as he remembered the look on her face in the store when she'd promised never to deal drugs or steal for him.

An hour later Basil rolled down both sleeves of his chambray shirt and walked into Jack's Village Tavern. He scanned the clumps of Crystal Springs locals as he crossed the room and claimed a stool at the end of the bar.

"What's your pleasure?" The bartender, a husky man in a plaid shirt, slapped a paper coaster in front of Basil.

"Liennie's original. Small." He parked one arm on the counter and rested his gaze on the pool players. A blond man with a prominent chin alternated shots with a teen who looked like a younger edition. Brothers. The game ended as the teen sank his final three balls in as many strokes.

"Remind me not to play you for money." The older brother put his cue in the wall rack before addressing the couple at the nearest table. "You want to give him a run, Brad? My mind's not on the game tonight."

Soft words bounced between the man in the long-sleeved T-shirt and the blond woman sipping a dark drink at his table.

"One game, Steve. Bragging rights, no cash."

The teen grinned and began to rack the balls.

Basil sipped beer and tuned in to the conversation between the bartender and the man leaving the pool table.

"Did the sheriff stop in at Farm Service today?" The bartender pulled two beers and one Diet Coke for the server.

"Sent a deputy. More questions on that list than a body could answer."

"Same here. They seem intent on tracing the steps of half a dozen people all the way from sunrise to midnight. What did you tell them, Sam?"

"The truth. Easier to remember that way. Pull me a Red." Sam glanced at the pool players before continuing. "Daniel came in that morning. So did Dray, Corey, and a dozen other people. If you want my opinion, I'd say half of them are smiling at the news Daniel's gone."

"Shouldn't speak ill of the dead." The barkeep handed him a glass with a perfect half inch of foam.

Sam glanced around and leaned a few inches closer. "According to chatter at the store, they found a drug lab in the barn."

"Explains the new truck. Any idea what will happen to it? It's a beauty."

Ingredients and equipment. I think I got all the finished product. Basil downed the last of his beer and tapped on the counter. "I'll have another. And the brat with kraut."

For the next half hour Basil dined on excellent bratwurst and sipped a second beer. He filed away bits of conversation and stray comments about Daniel from new arrivals and took special note when the server muttered a curse around the dead man's name. Maybe the chemist—make that late chemist—had made more enemies than Basil had given him credit for. In addition to Mr. Lincoln Dray, he'd rubbed someone named Corey the wrong way, and boasted of all the wrong things to the local businessmen.

A glint of metal from the pool table caught his attention. He'd kept his glances casual while the teen lost a quick game. Now the adult named Brad appeared to be giving a lesson. A cue slid across a metal hook at a perfect, low angle and sent two solids off to opposite pockets.

Small-town characters. Basil turned his attention to the attractive woman who had been with the one-armed man. She shared the table now with a man old enough to be her father and dressed like a preacher in black pants and white dress shirt. No, not a religious man; that clothing choice indicated something much worse.

He turned away and gulped the last of his beer. The only people in Basil's world that considered a tieless shirt casual dress were federal agents. Last thing he needed was to get dragged into conversation with a stray DEA busybody looking to cap his career with an exclamation point.

Basil slid a tip across the bar and made for the exit.

Chapter Twelve

Mona tapped the pristine number-ten envelope against her black twill pants. This morning, half an hour ago, she'd transferred her birth certificate from a mutilated manila container. I lucked out. She silently reviewed the highlights of the papers grabbed during her exit from the apartment.

She'd rescued birth certificates for both Matt and herself. She had her high school diploma, her parents' marriage certificate, and a letter to her grandmother signed by the Archbishop of St. Paul. A photocopy of her mother's life insurance, still awaiting payout, surprised her by being tucked inside a greeting card from her father.

"Are you still okay with this?" Linc pulled into a parking spot across from the courthouse.

"I'm good. I keep my promises." Will I regret this one?

"Glad to hear that. Sit tight a moment and I'll get your door like a polite fiancé."

The enormity, the finality, of the impending marriage license purchase pressed against her shoulders. She found a small, brave smile and waited for Linc to close up the van. When he laced his fingers with hers, warm confidence flooded in to nudge the blanket of doubt away. "Are you sure they're open?"

"Website said eight. It's a quarter past."

"Sounds like you want to be first in line."

"Promptness is a family trait. From what I understand, June tends to be a busy month for marriage licenses."

She nodded as they walked up the steps toward the main entrance. "And what other family traits go with punctuality?"

"You want the good ones or the questionable variety?"

"Let's put the whole thing on hold." She pointed to the directory board. "Room twenty-seven. Sounds like the basement."

A few moments later they stood side by side in front of an antique wooden counter while a clerk entered information into a very modern computer. Mona smoothed more wrinkles out of her birth certificate and placed her wallet ID on top.

"Have you made arrangements with the officiant?" The clerk returned their documents after entering the required data.

"Yes. The ceremony will be Monday, ten o'clock, with Benjamin Cobb." Linc gathered up his papers.

Mona brushed against his arm, blinked at the electric nature of such a small touch, and eased half a step away. She wanted all her senses to remain intact. This transaction was important to Linc's future. *And my own.* She pressed her lips tight and straightened her shoulders a fraction of an inch. Her decision was firm. She'd share the future with Linc as a friend and business associate. It didn't matter that they'd met less than a week ago. She sensed more stability in their relationship than in many marriages of her former co-workers.

"Raise your right hand, ma'am," the clerk prompted. "Mary Monica Smith, do you swear that the information given is true and correct? Do you further affirm there are no legal impediments to this marriage and you enter of your own free will, without coercion?"

"I do." Mona answered in a firm, strong voice.

"And you, sir." The clerk turned to Linc and repeated the oath.

"I...I...do."

Mona managed to constrain a bubbling laugh into a smile. Linc's hesitant, hoarse whisper contrasted with the confident man holding the door for her a mere twenty minutes ago.

Then signatures were collected, copies made, and a fee paid without comment to each other. The clerk handed their copy over, instructed them of the penalty for non-use within thirty days, and wished them a perfunctory good luck.

"Ready?" Mona touched his wrist.

He smiled for the first time since entering the office. "At your service."

"Lorraine asked that you bring me out to Polk Street today since our time frame was uncertain."

"After we go back to the house." Linc backed out of the parking space and merged into Tuesday-morning streets filled with commuters to nine o'clock deadlines. "I want to put our paperwork back in a safe place. I've got a locked drawer in the office desk if you want to put your things in it."

"Not today." *Does my new status give me entrance to the office?* While he'd never actually put the room off-limits in the same manner as his bedroom, he usually closed the door and projected an attitude that it was a private space. "The papers will be safe at Polk Street. Either Lorraine or I will be in the house one hundred percent of the time."

"Humor me. I've been in that house. Do you want to risk these getting mixed up with some of the six hundred other envelopes?"

"When you put it that way …"

She gazed off at traffic.

"The next time you have a few minutes," he said, "make a shopping list. Not groceries, more personal things." He turned to her while waiting for a traffic light. "I'm guessing you'll want a dress for the wedding. Or do you have one secreted away in your backpack?"

"You've pretty much seen my entire wardrobe." Except for the lingerie. Heat flashed up her neck. "I won't get anything fancy."

"We're here." He stated the obvious as he parked in front of the garage. "I'll run these inside. You sit tight for a minute."

Chapter Thirteen

"Your turn." Linc dismounted from the small green tractor and patted the seat. At least two hours of good daylight remained and he intended to make use of them. "Settle in here and I'll introduce you to John Deere."

"If you insist." Mona's silence and deliberate actions expressed more doubt about this project than pages of words.

"Better to start with this than the van. For all sorts of reasons." Insurance. Speed. Simplicity. The advantages clicked off in his mind as if part of a long master list. He didn't understand her hesitancy. She spoke of riding a twelve-speed bike in city traffic to school and her former job. The way he viewed it, that would make driving a four-speed tractor in an open area easy.

"Left foot controls the clutch. Press down on it. Check the action." He stood in the little wedge of space between the left rear wheel and the seat. "All the way. Don't be afraid to stretch your leg out."

"Stiff." She pressed all the way down and then jerked her foot back.

"Release it slowly." He watched her step off it like a hot rock again. "Did you ever take music lessons?"

"What's that got to do with driving?"

"Count slowly. Dirge tempo, as you release it. It helps one to not kill the engine or toss off passengers." He held back more instructions as she depressed and released the clutch twice more.

Pity he couldn't teach her the same way he'd learned. But he'd been a kid, sitting on Grandpa's lap, learning to steer and feel his way around while waiting for his legs to grow. He'd gained independence of a sort at age nine, when they let him drive with an empty hay wagon. He tamped down an image of Mona on his lap. Pictures like that damaged his concentration.

"What are all these other things?" She waved one hand across the control panel.

"One at a time." He moved around to the other side and explained the dual brakes.

A few minutes later he stepped on the drawbar and gripped the edge of her seat. He brushed against her shoulder and the pleasure made him glance down. She extended her left leg on the clutch, making a firm acquaintance with the very important pedal. "Ready for review? I'll name and you point."

"Steering wheel." She held it with both hands as she looked over her shoulder wearing a grin.

"First one correct." He relaxed half a notch. She was intelligent. He'd known that since the first night when she'd walked away rather than enter the house of an unknown man. "Throttle."

After the throttle and ignition he stepped off the drawbar and moved to the brake side. He hooked thumbs in back pockets to keep them from reaching out for her slender hand as she pointed and tapped. No matter how long in minutes this teaching session lasted it already felt like hours.

"Questions?"

"What's this short lever?" She rested her left hand on a smooth black knob for an instant.

"Power take-off. We won't be using it today. Not for a long time, actually."

"What does it do?"

He exhaled, patted a rear tire, and hunted for an explanation that might fit her experience. "Turns a connector. Powers other equipment. Like the mower."

She adjusted her pale blue cap and nodded. "Ignore."

"Anything else?" He took his place on the drawbar and searched for a firm hold on the sides of the seat. "Shift in neutral? Step on the clutch and turn the key."

Grrrr. Pop. Her hand flew away from the key before the engine caught.

"Again." He forced calm into the word.

One more false start and two clutch releases that almost threw him off his perch, and they rolled forward. He instructed her to follow the orchard fence in low gear at one third throttle. He talked her through a corner and got her settled into a nice large oval in the unplanted half of the fenced area. "Check your front wheel. Ignore the gopher mounds. Now stop."

She pushed the clutch in one smooth motion.

"Reverse."

"What?"

"Put it in reverse. The 'R' in the pattern." He conquered the urge to reach across her arm and move the lever.

She moved the gear shift and released the clutch with a jerk.

He clung tight to the seat and leaned forward, fighting for patience. "Look over your shoulder. Turn the wheel to the right before you get to the fence."

"Yes, sir."

He felt every ripple under the wheels during a sweeping turn. One glance off to his left showed the fence a good three feet away. He relaxed half a degree.

"Turn right again. Straighten the wheel." With his lips only inches from her right ear he spoke in a conversational tone, the steady throb of the engine no serious competition. "Stop. Low gear. Easy with the foot."

They did circles and figure eights in forward and reverse until their merged shadow elongated to the credits of a monster cartoon. "Follow the fence and take us to the main gate."

"Company?" She turned her face for an instant, her knuckles white and forcing the wheel steady.

"Neighbor." It looked like Corey. He didn't see a vehicle so figured the man stopped in during one of his cross-country walks. On Wednesday? He worked second shift, didn't he? When they pulled even to the gate post he told Mona to stop. "Turn it off." Sudden silence was broken by one person clapping. "Put it in a gear, any gear. You did good."

Linc lingered by the rear of the tractor, holding his smile to small until Mona discovered a way down from her seat. A moment later she walked stiff-legged toward him, rubbing her bottom. "Yeah. It feels cushioned for five minutes or less." He wrapped his arm around her shoulders and drew her close for a light kiss on the cheek. He longed to give her a proper reward, but they had an audience. "Let's introduce you to Corey Maxwell."

"Patti's gone." Corey spit out the statement after giving Mona's hand a brief shake.

"When?" Linc pulled Mona nearer to his side. Patti was Corey's wife, third wife, much younger and rumored to be giving Daniel more than dancing lessons.

"Today?" Corey missed the horizontal bar on the gate with his foot, caught it on the second try, and perched a work boot in a cowboy pose. "No. Last night."

"Is this the first time?" Linc studied the other man's hands. They looked steady enough, but the more Corey drank the less he talked. And words appeared to be slow for him at the moment.

Corey shrugged, paused, and appeared to think hard. "Went to her sister."

Linc waited, rubbed Mona's shoulder, and prayed she'd stay silent. He doubted an intoxicated Corey would take well to interruptions by a stranger.

"We got into it before I went to work." Corey lifted his shoulders and clung to the gate with both hands. "Patti. Music. Men."

"Give her time," Linc suggested. *I should talk. What did Mona have? Thirty-six, forty-eight hours?*

"She cheated." Corey leaned forward, enveloping his words in stale beer scent. "Lawyers will take it all. Man can't come out even."

Linc glanced between Mona and Corey. His neighbor was in bad shape, acting as if he'd not added any food to his drink all day. At least he didn't try to drive.

"Tango. Tangled. In my own damn bed. Daniel deserved his beating."

Linc gazed toward yellow tape still across the barn doors. Either Corey knew something important or the alcohol told a good story. All he'd managed to get out of the sheriff's department was little bits of information. They acknowledged that Daniel's body was discovered on the doorstep of his shed, in a tarp they took into evidence. A mixture of official facts and rumors pointed to illegal drug manufacturing in the barn. Cause of death was being held close by law enforcement. Yet Corey spoke with certainty of a beating. "I tolerated him. No big secret we weren't friends."

"Nope. No secret." Corey took notice of Mona with a nod and a crooked smile. "You been in the barn, little lady?"

"Sheriff's got it off limits." She squeezed Linc's hand.

"Clever set-up. Generator and everything. Want to see?" Corey pushed the gate open further.

"Not today."

"Corey," Linc interrupted the exchange. "How about we drive you home?"

"Patti's gone."

"You're drunk, Mr. Maxwell." Mona pushed past him and opened the van's side door. "You belong at home. In bed."

"You coming with?"

"Dirty old man."

Linc gave her a nod and a thumbs-up sign.

* * *

Mona swung her arm to direct Corey to the open van door. "Come sit, Mr. Maxwell."

Corey studied her and raised an index finger to his temple. "Not old."

"Drunk." She managed only the single word before Linc started the tractor. She shrugged at the complication to conversation. Tipsy customers at the diner didn't make for many rational exchanges. All too often they came in after the bars closed, demanded coffee, and grabbed at her arm as she poured. Unpredictable.

Linc emerged from the shed after parking the tractor and sent several glances in her direction as he closed the doors and snapped a new combination lock into place. "Time to go home, Corey."

The drunk released his hold on the gate and took several uneven steps before sinking down in the van. He grabbed an assist handle, kept both feet on the ground, and looked at Mona. "I'm not old. Fifty. A month ago."

"Inside, old man." She stared at his one day growth of salt-and-pepper beard. "Fifty makes you older than my father."

"Bossy. Pretty. Come home with me?"

She reached down, surrounded his knees, and lifted his legs into the van before he reached for her. "Settle in."

"Listen to her, Corey." Linc blocked the drunk's arms. "I'm taking you home. Best offer you're going to get."

"You vomit in the van, you clean it." Mona stepped away to tend the gate.

"She's right. Now grab hold on the console or something." Linc closed the sliding door, gave Mona a nod of approval, and climbed in the driver's seat.

"Thief," Corey said as Mona got into the passenger seat. "Bad seed."

Is he babbling about Daniel?

"Hang on, pothole coming up."

"Stole my Patti," Corey continued.

Mona opened her mouth and closed it before the first question could escape. Mr. Maxwell wasn't rational at the moment. She'd save the multiplying questions for Linc during the forty-odd miles back to Eau Claire.

"Last stop." Linc halted the van several yards from the back porch of a two-story house centered on a neat yard.

Mona got out and pushed back the side door. "Time to get out, Mr. Maxwell."

His legs and body moved stiff and awkward until his feet touched the ground and his fingers found a plastic handle. "This ain't Jack's."

"Home." Linc guided Corey's head away from obstacles as he pulled him to his feet and shouldered in for support.

"Keys." Mona held out her hand to the pair of men.

"Try the door," Linc suggested. "I'm not going to frisk him until I know it's locked."

She crossed the open porch and frowned at five empty beer cans lined up at the end. A moment later she stood inside the storm door and tested the main entrance. The knob turned easily. Stale beer, onions, and unwashed socks scented the cluttered kitchen. *I've smelled worse.* Empty Leinenkugal cans lay dented on the counter and she glimpsed more in the top layer of the trash can.

Linc guided a stumbling Corey past her and into the next room.

"Are you putting him to bed?"

"Sofa," Linc replied. "All the bedrooms are upstairs."

"Do you plan to leave him?" She stood at the edge of the room as Linc lowered a silent Corey to a brown vinyl couch.

"He'll be fine."

"I counted fifteen empties in plain sight." Mona stepped forward and started to unlace Corey's boots. As she tugged the braided nylon loose, she glanced at the side of the boot she touched and then Linc's. "Check this."

"Red Wing boots? Nothing odd about that. Wear them myself."

"I see that." She shrugged, but the memory of Linc giving his boot prints to the crime scene technician lingered.

Linc stuffed a throw pillow from a recliner under Corey's head. "He'll sleep it off. Be good as normal by morning. Hope he remembers to go to work tomorrow afternoon."

"Does he do this often?" She handed Linc an afghan from the back of a rocker.

"He has a reputation. I haven't witnessed much firsthand." He shook the crocheted blanket and let it settle over the sleeping man. "He's off the roads and not wandering around the fields in the dark. Nothing more we can do for him."

Mona paused in the kitchen. "Do you know Patti? Should we call her? Is she the sort of person to come back?"

"I don't have the first clue where to contact her." Linc touched her elbow. "It's time for us to go home."

Us. Home. She led the way to the van as the coded conversation of a drunken neighbor refused to vanish.

Chapter Fourteen

Mona tested the gold ring past her knuckle over and over. The slender new band glided easy. "Fits well. Yours?"

"Exactly as advertised." Linc eased off his matching ring and tucked it into the small square box.

"They can share." She slipped off the gold band and set it on the Dacron pad next to his. Any moment now she expected the dream to snap and she'd wake, scrubbing restaurant pots in a steamy room.

Instead she blinked twice and still heard reluctant shopping cart wheels. Parent commands to children drifted in from other regions of the mega discount store. Fresh popcorn scent invaded from the snack bar and settled sweeter than dessert in her stomach.

Friday. She hooked uncooperative hair behind her ear and forced a smile for Linc. A casual observer would see a groom on a budget paying for wedding rings. This hurried marriage with deadlines, short acquaintance, and the inheritance of a family farm in the balance didn't break past his calm exterior. No. Once, in the clerk's office, he showed hesitation. She looked away, afraid he'd read something on her face. She needed to emphasize the positive, not dredge up his stumbles through the oath.

"Are you ready to do serious shopping?" He touched her hand.

He's playacting the groom again. She refused to dwell on the warm comfort that invaded from his fingertips all the way to her core. In an effort to mask his true effect on her she straightened and stepped away from the glass counter. "You don't need to do this. You already bought your own ring."

He shrugged. "I want to. And I think you deserve a new dress and any little accessory doodads that come with it."

"I have a little of my own money. Plus Lorraine paid me today."

"Enough?" He held her hand, lightly, but impossible to ignore. "It's your wedding. My experience with brides is limited, but I gathered the impression they liked to be fancy."

"That's not the question. Yes, I'd like to get married in a dress. And I didn't think to bring one when I left. That doesn't mean you need to pay for it." She added the advertised price of sundresses they'd walked past and a few other basics lacking in her backpack for one reason or another. She could make it with all of her wages for the week and only a few dollars out of her reserves.

"I'm going to go for a haircut." He forced several bills into her hand. "I'll meet you in the front. Look for me on one of those old-men benches outside the optical shop in an hour or so. Fair enough?"

"I'll add a few staples for the house." It didn't feel right for the groom to buy her dress. No matter how the reasons for this marriage—business deal, farce—tilted toward him.

A short time later, Mona emerged from the fitting room, added the cream, red, and black sundress to her cart, and headed toward accessories. A red purse with an adjustable strap fit her needs and budget as the next addition. She tossed in a package of socks on the way past the display and rounded the corner to shoes.

She owned sandals, loafers, wedges, three pairs of boots, and two pairs of sneakers. The problem at the moment was that the sneakers on her feet and worn flip-flops at the duplex were the only shoes not tumbled in the Minneapolis closet. They could have been on the moon for all the use they did at the moment. She reached for a delicate white sandal with a three-inch heel. Bargain price. A minute later she pulled out a pair of size fives and smiled. It was time to head for the more practical aisles: cleaning supplies, beauty, and health.

Laundry stain remover, a package of sponges, and toothpaste dropped from her hands into the cart after minimum decisions. Need these. She placed a box of tampons beside the new shoes. Four steps further down the aisle, she paused to let another shopper through and stared at the display on her right.

She gripped the cart handle and considered the boxes with bold, heroic brand names. What sort of wedding night did Linc plan? Did he keep condoms at the house? Leftovers from—Tami?

She reached out and then retracted her hand the instant it grazed the box of twelve. It wouldn't be the first time she'd purchased them. Like a careful twenty-first century girl she'd carried a pair in her purse for years. Hadn't needed one since—last fall, or a year ago?

Then Linc's kiss invaded her memory. She'd never been affected by a kiss like that before. She'd never felt such a perfect fit, or wanted so much from a man's mouth. Every night since Monday the tingle from it crawled into bed with her, tickled her mind, and interfered with nightly prayers.

We get married Monday. The pastor of a small independent church had promised a short ceremony with the traditional vows. Mona steered her cart into the next aisle and stared without seeing at the shampoo display. What's going to happen after the wedding kiss?

* * *

Basil stood two paces away from Nick and gave a second look to each of the teens and young adults as they entered the warehouse. The dance floor was getting crowded with laughter and shouts competing with a band of drums, two guitars, and a saxophone. My last one.

He reached for his phone before the chirp announcing a text faded. He read the single word from his spotter and swore before holding up the message for Nick. "Raid!"

"Damn!" Nick echoed and grabbed the most recent arrival by the arm. "Sorry, man, we're closed."

Basil headed into the mass of swaying bodies, turned a few around, and pointed them toward the door. "Scat." At the base of the small stage he gave hand signals to the lead guitarist and waited while he morphed the band into a slow tempo rendition of "Get Lucky."

Each and every employee understood what that song meant: open the exits, thin the crowd, and dump drugs.

Basil did his share of pushing dancers toward one of the three alley exits suddenly opened. He aimed for his office. Unknown to even Nick, he intended to stuff tonight's receipts into his pockets and melt into the dark city night.

A young girl in a pink tube top threw both arms around Basil's neck. "Dance with me, big boy."

"Leave." He disengaged her hands and turned her toward the nearest exit. He pushed her toward a boy with neck tattoos. "Follow him. You'll thank me in the morning."

"Quitter." She reached for his arm but he evaded it.

She looks twelve. I'm getting too old for this. He continued to move across the dance floor, directing people out. A scream erupted at the front entrance.

"Brute."

"We have a warrant. Hands up. Face the wall."

Damn and double damn. Not my night. Basil pushed his way through the remaining crowd until he sighted a female patron held tight by two officers wearing riot helmets. "Ease up. All of you."

"You." A tall man pointed to Basil with a baton. "With the others."

Basil glimpsed federal agency initials across the officer's jacket as a strong hand pushed him against the wall. An instant later his skin shivered under the familiar pattern of a frisk. He'd avoid a weapons charge; he never carried during a rave. Who snitched? "ID's in right back pocket. Sir."

Chapter Fifteen

Mona rubbed her thumb across the keys and new fob from Linc. She held the duplex key up to the morning sunshine admitted to her room from the single window. This most recent gift from him symbolized so much: trust from him, independence for her. A smile tugged the end of her mouth upward as she dangled the molded acrylic decoration in the light. A bright red apple and two green leaves molded flat changed sunlight into bright geometrics on a white wall. Fake stained glass.

"He trusts me." She glanced at the two framed photos on the small table. "I'm sorry you can't see me as a bride, Mother. He's a good man. I don't know if I love him … it's all rushed. I'll do my best. Forgive my mistakes."

She touched the top of the second frame, the one with cracked glass. "Granny, you tried all our time together to teach me right. I'll not be speaking my marriage vows in what you consider a sacred space. I do remember your lessons in my heart. Bless me."

A moment later, she dropped the keys into her new purse. They nestled beside the cell phone and bus pass, the other recent signs of progress and independence. She swallowed hard at the memory of more keys Linc wanted to add. Learning to drive is important to him. Just last night, over his ritual dish of ice cream, he'd talked of driving lessons, of getting her license and perhaps a used car before they moved to the farm. Her mind stalled in confusion thinking that far ahead.

One hour until the wedding. She'd be—Mrs. Lincoln Dray? Mary Monica Dray? Mona Smith? *I'll keep my name.* She recalled Linc's raised eyebrows when she'd stated her decision, but he'd voiced no objection. No, he'd expanded her name in private to, Mary Monica "call me Mona" Smith. She didn't feel capable of adding an identity change to her life today. Thank goodness, the official legal records would not be affected by a delay.

Door chimes interrupted the soft house sounds. She dropped the tissue packet in her hand before she identified the three tuned notes.

"I'll get it." Linc's voice drifted down. A moment later his footsteps in dress shoes slapped against the upper flight of steps.

Mona heard male voices, low pitched, the words lost in the wide space of lower level. She practiced a smile in case Daryl had decided to meet them here instead of at the chapel.

"Mona."

"On my way." She gripped the purse in one hand and hurried as fast as her new, still unfamiliar, three-inch-heeled sandals allowed.

"What?" She snapped her mouth shut before another word escaped. Two sheriff's deputies stood in the foyer and another pair waited a few steps outside, on the flat cement square of an entrance.

"Mary Smith?" The largest uniformed officer addressed her.

She clasped her purse tight enough to whiten her knuckles. "Yes."

"We have warrants." He waved a handful of folded papers. At his nod another officer stepped inside and reached for first one and then the other of Linc's wrists. "Lincoln Dray, you are under arrest for the murder of Daniel Larson."

"No!" Mona leaned forward and sealed her mouth shut. Police didn't listen during an arrest. Sometimes they remained deaf to reason too long.

"We have evidence that proves you attacked Mr. Larson in the barn." The officer with the papers beckoned a woman forward. "Fingerprint match came back this morning."

"Ms. Smith."

Mona turned toward the female voice only to be confronted with another deputy. The woman grasped her hand, handed her purse to another officer, and continued to place handcuffs on Mona.

"Mary Monica Smith, you are under arrest for obstruction of justice in the murder of Daniel Larson. You have the right—"

Voices blurred to a murmur as Mona watched one officer open her purse and thumb through the contents while another frisked Linc for weapons. Uniforms and faces blurred through unshed tears. She blinked the world back into focus and lifted her chin. Linc was innocent. She was innocent. She pressed her lips tight. Best not to give any words for the police to twist against them later.

"Place them in separate cars."

"I see one pair of boots." An officer eased past Mona to the collection of Linc's shoes on a rug.

"Check all the rooms and closets for a second pair."

Mona moved forward into the sunshine without warmth or promise. She halted when the deputy tugged on her arm and brought the scene into clarity. A parade of police cruisers, two from River County Sheriff Department and one from the City of Eau Claire, lined the narrow street. She glanced down the row and spotted a crime scene van and a black sedan bristling with antenna. Everything except a SWAT team. Linc stood mere yards away under the watchful eye of one officer while he consulted with two others.

Scattered words from this low conversation reached her out of context: lawyer, witness, procedure.

"No. No. No. You have it all wrong." She spewed the words out as a deputy escorted her to the second patrol car.

"Calm down, ma'am." He opened the rear door and placed his hand on the top of her head.

"White," Linc called to her from outside the lead car. "My lawyer … our lawyer's name is White. In Wagoner."

Our? Mona held her breath while the officer fastened the seat belt. She had debt and no job. How could she even dream of money for an attorney? All her nightmares piled atop each other, leaving only cracks and slivers of a fine June morning. She opened her mouth to scream and swallowed it back at the last instant as handcuff chains clinked on her lap.

"Sit tight." The officer closed the door on her world.

What choice do I have? After three deep, calming breaths she looked out from her cocoon in the back seat. The officers held another conversation complete with wide gestures from the largest, most authoritative one. They finished placing Linc in the car ahead of her and she fixed her gaze on the back of his head. Our lawyer's name is White. She leaned forward, tested the range of the seat belt, and studied her feet. Last night she'd applied bright red polish to her toenails as a symbol of joy, luck, and the beginning of new life. Laughter begged for release and sent a ripple over her skin.

"Ready." The female officer slipped in beside Mona while another deputy took the driver's seat.

Mona struggled to keep her expression serious and quiet while they followed the other patrol car to the freeway. Soon they traveled west at the speed limit; Eau Claire with its small comforts and promises shrank by the moment. She stared at the car ahead, the one carrying Linc. What was he thinking? His absolute deadline to be married was midnight tomorrow. Would they be in jail?

"Excuse me, officer." Mona dampened her lips and risked a question. "This judge we'll end up in front of today. Does he do marriages?"

* * *

Why? Why? Why? Linc sealed his lips while the question of the moment ran laps in his brain. The sheriff thought he killed Daniel? What sort of fake evidence had prompted this arrest? And Mona? He closed his eyes for a long moment, as if that could blot out his final glimpse of her, standing bewildered next to the second patrol car.

"You okay, mister? Not going to get sick?" The deputy sharing the back seat of the cruiser broke the silence.

Linc opened his eyes and gazed at green western Wisconsin scenery flowing past for a full minute.

"I'm okay." Physically. "I won't vomit all over your car."

If mental confusion counted as an illness he'd be in critical condition. But he could control the physical part so far. The thing he refused to do was to be drawn into conversation during the drive. At the first opportunity he'd use his phone call to contact Wayne White. The family attorney usually handled wills, trusts, and real-estate transactions, but the man had contacts.

He shifted his gaze to his shoes and attempted to think of something pleasant. Breakfast with Mona returned as a warm memory. He could almost see her hands wrapped around her white coffee mug, bright red polished nails on full display.

"Pretty," he'd complimented her.

"It's a bride thing. Red represents good luck and happiness in Chinese culture."

"Should I wear my red tie? Will it bring luck and joy to the groom?" He couldn't stop a big grin.

"Almost there, Mr. Dray. I expect Sheriff Bergstrom will want to ask the questions today." The deputy's words brought Linc back to the present.

He took a few deep breaths as he planned his first minutes out of the car. He tried to remember if Mr. White's business card was in his wallet. He stared off in the direction of the lawyer's office, trying to remember if Wayne's father, the senior partner of White and White, specialized in criminal cases. Would they accept Mona as a client? His hands trembled until the chains clinked at the thought of her getting a public defender at some sort of River County Bar Association lottery.

As they turned into the small lot behind the two-story brick sheriff's office and jail, he turned his head and sealed his lips against a curse. The second patrol car, the one carrying Mona, was nowhere in sight.

Half an hour later, Linc waited in a small office. The silver globe in the corner of the ceiling hinted at camera surveillance. He turned his face away from its unblinking eye and thought back to discussions with his brother. Jackson's criminal law courses had furnished lots of conversation between the brothers during Christmas break three years ago. The less I say, the better. He looked across the ultra-tidy desk and counted the carved pigs on two small shelves. Fourteen, just like the last time he'd counted them, an entire three, maybe four minutes ago. The collection of wooden figures hadn't changed.

He stared down at his hands, counted the links between the metal cuffs around his wrists. Nope, that number hadn't changed either.

Where are you, Mona? Are you frightened? He recalled her quiet, uncomfortable demeanor after the initial interview on the farm. She didn't like cops or lawyers. He blew out a lungful of air. He couldn't help that she'd see too many of both today. He mouthed a silent combination prayer and wish for her to be calm, strong, and brave.

He turned his head toward the door as two voices in conversation approached. A shadow, or an arm, moved outside the narrow window above the doorknob. He allowed a little hope that this time the elder Mr. White would be his lawyer.

"Mr. Dray?" A trim man with milk white hair and a goatee to match walked into the room carrying a large battered briefcase.

"Yes." He stood out of respect. "Are you Clarence White?"

"Correct. My son described your case to me." He took the second visitor chair in the room and motioned Linc to sit. "We—my son and I—will work together. He's making a few calls before starting his interview with Miss Mary Smith. Tell me about her."

"In twenty words or less?"

"I'm an attorney. No word limit."

Linc relaxed and smiled. Like his son, this elderly man demonstrated a knack for putting a client at ease in difficult situations. "She likes to be called Mona. Our wedding was scheduled for this morning. Ten o'clock."

"Ahhh. Your nuptials will be postponed. But I'll do what I can to get you out of here as soon as possible."

"I didn't kill Daniel Larson. He and I held different opinions on all sorts of things. But I didn't hurt him." Linc looked away from the attorney and stared at the camera. The sparse explanation from the deputies this morning returned to run another lap around his skull. *How could we have killed Daniel in the barn? We never set foot in it that day.*

"Good. It's much easier when the client is innocent." Mr. White removed a yellow pad from his case and began to take notes. "No acting, Mr. Dray. Sheriff Bergstrom assured me the camera and microphone will remain off while you and I have a good chat."

* * *

Mona listened to voices in muffled conversation beyond the door of a small, sparse room. Four plain metal chairs and a rectangular table bolted to the floor matched concrete walls covered with pale tan paint. The dreary color complemented her mood of confusion coating fear. She identified the speakers as two men and a woman, but failed to capture more than a stray word of the exchange.

Keep me out of it. She tipped her face to the camera near the ceiling and sealed her mouth into a neutral expression. Would they send her a lawyer? She recalled her brother's most recent public defender and shivered. Overworked. Inexperienced. Eager to cut a deal and avoid a trial. She listed all the things she didn't want but her brother had suffered through.

This is different. I'm innocent.

She looked at the floor and replayed her one phone call in her mind. Had she wasted her opportunity by leaving a message for Daryl Frieberg? The wedding should have been over by the time she left the voice mail. Would he understand her scrambled message, a mixture of information and plea for help? And she counted on him to share with the clergyman, Ben Cobb. Then there was Dr. and Lorraine Terrier. They'd interrupted their day to witness vows, not wait in a chapel for a bride and groom now sitting miles away—in shackles.

Another lock of hair fell forward. She started to raise a hand to hook it behind her ear and found another reminder of her captivity in the clink of the handcuffs. Bosh on all of them. She lifted both hands and swept the wayward hair back into place.

"Miss Smith?" A thick-set man of middle age invaded the room and extended a hand. "Wayne White. Attorney at Law. My father and I will be your defense team."

"Have you seen Linc? How is he?" Her words escaped before she could bring her hands off her lap.

"He's talking with my father…" He angled one of the empty chairs to make it easier for them to talk. "Camera's off. I need honest and complete answers from you. I don't want any surprises when the detective comes in for the formal interrogation."

She tensed at his word choice. "Neither Linc nor I had anything to do with a murder."

"Good start." He set a blank pad and pen within easy reach. "Mr. Frieberg shared only a little background information with me. Tell me all about your relationship with Lincoln Dray."

"Linc and I should be married by now." She stared at Mr. White's wrist and read the time from his watch. "An hour ago."

"Continue." He scribbled two words on paper.

"Linc helped me leave Minneapolis," Mona began. "A criminal gang leader broke into my apartment on Thursday and left an obvious threat. I needed to get space between us and give him a chance to cool off. I spotted Linc at the airport and begged a ride. After that …" She hesitated and watched the lawyer touch his pen to a new line. "He offered room and board for housekeeping. I accepted, strictly temporarily, but he had other ideas."

"Skip to Saturday," Mr. White prodded.

"We went to the orchard after a stop in town. I went to the convenience store and Linc picked up some sort of spray at the farm supply. Then we drove out to the farm and started working. Neither of us left the fenced area until late afternoon." She clenched her hands tight at the memory of the marriage proposal over lunch. Enough events for a lifetime crowded on top of each other in less than a week. "We met Daryl Frieberg and Kathy Miller for supper at the tavern."

"And you went directly into town after you put the tools in the shed?" Mr. White glanced at his watch as if their allotted time was soon to expire.

"We did. On the way ... almost to town ... we were passed by Basil headed toward the farm."

"Who?"

"Basil Berg. He deals in drugs, stolen goods, and prostitution in Minneapolis. He's the reason I left the Cities. I thought he'd found Linc's van and was still after me."

"Why would he follow you all that way?"

"One of his informants lied to him—told him I was holding out money from a robbery committed by my brother."

"Is he still looking for you?"

"He found me." She studied the ceiling for a long moment before returning her gaze to the lawyer. "Sunday afternoon he tracked me down. We got straight on the money. But ... he didn't want it known he was in Crystal Springs on Saturday."

"Anything else I need to know? I hate surprises in front of police."

"My brother's in prison. Will they use it against me?" She didn't know how large a shadow his history would cast.

"Should they?"

"No. I left Minneapolis to protect him." She shook her head and stared at the lawyer's face. On another person she'd call it honest, inviting trust. But she disliked his profession and retreated a mental step. "Can you protect Matt?"

"He's in prison. Who's after him?"

Mona moved her gaze to the camera, swallowed hard, and prayed both video and audio feed remained disconnected. "His former boss, Basil Berg. His minions welcomed him to prison with a beating."

"I'll do what I can. In a few minutes the senior detective in the county will walk through that door and start his questions. If he touches on anything you don't want to answer I'll help you shut it down. Fair enough?"

"I can't pay you."

"We'll sort that out later. First we try to get the charges dropped or bail set."

She didn't have funds to pay bail. She inspected her hands and considered how the prison orange would clash with the Tart Cherry Red on her nails. It didn't look pretty.

Chapter Sixteen

Linc walked in small, uncertain steps behind the deputy. Ankle cuffs shortened his usual stride and with the additional chain running up to his waist and beyond to his wrists he felt like a stooped-over old man. He hadn't been this conscious of each step since his final semester in college, when he'd smashed his left foot and hobbled for weeks in a fracture boot.

He paused at the bottom of six wide concrete steps. One quick glance over his shoulder confirmed Mona followed two yards behind. He stopped a greeting in his throat as the deputy next to her sent him a stern look. No talking. He stared at her, silently begging her to make eye contact. There, for an instant, he attempted a smile and received a small shake of her head.

"Move along." The deputy beside him touched his elbow.

Linc lifted one shower-sandaled foot with care and climbed toward the open door.

Cool air, scented with decades of lemon furniture polish and masculine aftershave, replaced the sunshine and new-mown grass of a moment ago. Links of his chain clinking against each other destroyed a fantasy of sitting on a bench outside to soak up fresh air. It was well into the afternoon and since his morning ride in the back of a patrol car he'd been in one or another of small rooms with too many bodies and voices.

"Wait here." The lead deputy brought their small parade to a halt on the second floor, beside an unmarked wood door.

Linc nodded and scanned the hall. They stood beneath fluorescent tube lighting suspended from a high ceiling wearing tired white paint. He considered leaning against the wall but discarded the idea in favor of another glimpse of Mona. She stood still, appeared tiny in the tall corridor.

"All set." The officer returned and opened the door.

Soft voices hushed to deep silence the instant Linc stepped across the threshold into the courtroom.

He looked straight ahead and moved one foot after another where the deputy indicated. Clink. Clink. Jingle.

His chains indicated his progress to the table where Mr. White and his son stood, their conversation interrupted. He nodded at the lawyers and listened to Mona's restraints echo his own as she shuffled and clinked off to his left.

"Do we need those?" Clarence White pointed to the restraints and addressed the lead officer in a harsh whisper.

"Judge's order."

Mr. White frowned at the deputy and motioned Linc to sit. "The judge watches too many movies. You may not need to speak at all. If you do, keep it short and formal."

"Yes, sir." Linc nodded to his own lawyer while allowing his gaze to follow Wayne White to the jury seating where Mona sat at the near end of the first row. Be kind to her.

"Prosecutor will try to keep you in jail. Less reaction from you while I negotiate bail works better." Clarence White kept his voice hushed.

Linc nodded understanding. Following directions and listening were his primary duties in this room. He took a moment while his lawyer arranged papers on the table to look at the spectator benches. Three people, none of them familiar, waited.

"All stand." The bailiff announced the court session and introduced the judge.

Linc turned forward, stood, and laced his fingers. He glimpsed a man at a second table littered with manila folders. The prosecutor? The man looked fit and in his prime. How difficult would he make an old man's negotiations?

"Be seated." The judge settled into a high-backed chair between national and state flags. He appeared to move papers around on a sunken portion of the bench.

Linc remained aware of every clink of his restraints as he took his seat. He felt as obvious as sitting on bubble wrap in church.

The clerk stood, read the case number, and ordered the principals in Dray vs. State of Wisconsin to rise.

Linc levered up, and slid his gaze toward Mona. She appeared calm from this vantage point. He didn't want to think about his own lack of acting skill.

"Approach." The judge beckoned the attorneys and defendant forward.

Linc straightened his shoulders and studied the judge during the short walk. The man wore a closed businesslike expression.

"To the charge of second-degree intentional homicide, how do you plead?"

He blinked and glanced toward his lawyer.

"My client pleads not guilty, Your Honor." Clarence White's voice emerged strong and clear to fill the entire room.

"So entered. And to the accompanying charges, how do you plead?"

"Not guilty." The exchange repeated between Clarence White and the judge.

"Your Honor." The prosecutor held tight to one slim manila folder. "Due to the nature of the charges and both physical and circumstantial evidence against the accused, the people request bond be set at one million dollars."

Linc clenched his hands, fighting the body blow in the words. Did the old man beside him stand a chance for a reasonable amount?

"The defense requests release on his own recognizance, Your Honor." Mr. White's voice dropped in volume but stayed determined. "The accused has no history of violence. He is employed with strong ties to this part of Wisconsin. My client does not pose a flight risk."

"Your Honor," the prosecutor countered.

Linc stared at the American flag behind the judge and listened to the lawyers volley his fate like a tennis ball. The two attorneys were a generation apart but after several lobs their voices sounded remarkably similar.

"Gentlemen." The judge brought the room to a hush with one tap of his gavel.

"Bail shall be set at two hundred and fifty thousand dollars, cash or bond, and the defendant's passport surrendered."

Linc stood perfectly still. He couldn't breathe; the weight of a quarter million dollars crushed his chest.

"Next case." The judge broke the murmur from the spectators.

"Mr. Dray." Clarence White placed one hand on his shoulder and directed him to the deputy at the far end of the jury seating. "I'll make the necessary calls."

"Smith versus the State of Wisconsin."

Linc listened through a fog to a replay of his recent drama with a different voice volleying against the prosecutor. With each blink and breath from his new vantage point the scene clarified until he listened for Mona's voice.

"Fifty thousand, ten percent cash, and surrender your passport." The judge struck the gavel. "This hearing stands adjourned."

Linc struggled to his feet with the rest of the assembly as the judge gathered several files into a bundle and exited. Physical and circumstantial evidence? He and Mona had left fingerprints all over the tools in the shed. How did anything tie either of them to the activity inside the barn?

He remained in place and scanned the room. Clarence and Wayne White joined the prosecutor studying a paper. A deputy prodded Mona into motion. She's pale. He moved a foot to go to her and a muted rattle reminded him of his bonds.

"Time to go. Need to get you back before supper is served." A deputy spoke from a step away. "No talking until we're back at the jail."

* * *

Mona shrank in the corner of the bench and wrapped both arms around her body. The small portion of mediocre meatloaf and mashed potatoes she'd managed to eat congealed like wet sand in her stomach. At least the attendant removed the tray without a comment. She tipped her head back against cool painted concrete, and reviewed the hearing.

"Don't worry. I'll take care of it." She repeated Wayne White's parting words to the quiet women's cell of River County jail. The lawyer in the courtroom was serious and formal. In the interview before and during the detective's interrogation he presented cheerfulness with efficiency. But the big questions remained.

How did the pry bar with her prints get from the tool shed to the barn? When did Linc's boots make prints on the drug lab floor? Did Mr. White believe her theory including Basil? Did he actually think he would be paid for his time today? Bail, even ten percent of the amount the judge pronounced from the bench, equaled a hundred times more than the balance in her Minneapolis bank account. Never mind she didn't have current access to even that small amount.

If I had five thousand dollars ... She sighed. Money in excess of her recent trip to the discount store belonged in mirages. She thought back to only a few weeks ago. Then she brainstormed with a friend and created a plan to live bare bones until her mother's final medical bills were paid off. Her friend

Jennifer agreed to charge her one-third of the rate at the apartment. It wouldn't be pleasant watching every penny. But her family had coped with hard times before. She knew how to make one tea bag last all day, rinse out the shampoo bottle, and wear clothes until they disintegrated at the Laundromat.

"Then I visited Matt. Basil threatened me. And poof, panic takes my life path and flips it around until it's snarled beyond recognition." She pushed to her feet and paced an oval in her cell. Sandals three sizes too large slapped with each step. Do they have real evidence? Linc deserves better.

Male voices seeped through the cement wall from the men's cells. She listened but failed to catch any actual words. After a minute or two she separated out three distinct voices, none of them Linc. How was he doing? He'd looked confused in the courtroom. She wrapped her arms around her torso, pretended she'd been able to give Linc a hug, a touch, a genuine smile during those brief moments. No matter what happened next, even if she aged in a cell like this, she would not blame him. If anything, he should be blaming her. She was the one who brought trouble in her wake.

A few minutes later, as she unfolded the single blanket and prepared to make her bed for the night, a new sound invaded. Loud, coarse words fitted loosely to "The City of New Orleans" escaped from the men's side of the jail.

"Knock it off."
"Who told you to sing?"
"My dog carries a tune better."

The next exchanges dropped lower until they became muffled rumbles.

Mona retreated into her own mind. Who was the singer? Linc? No—according to the Tim McGraw song leaking out of the shower the other morning, he sang average or better. Would the other men harm him?

Her face warmed as memories from their conversation over breakfast surfaced. She glanced down at her red nails, noticed a few tiny chips along the edges. Tonight—she swallowed hard—should be my ... his ... our wedding night. They—or at least she—didn't have special plans made. But officially it would mark their first night as a married couple.

A legal marriage. Was it her gift to Linc? Yes, you can put my name on a certificate to get land for your orchard.

And what did she receive? He'd offered protection. Yeah, like that happened. She could alibi him. Did they listen? She snorted. Law enforcement followed their own selective observations. Officials in uniforms must assume she and Linc both lied.

She perched on the edge of her bed and let her imagination work on the story that someone created out of nothing to get them here, in jail for murder and obstruction. The only story that formed in her mind—Linc left me in the orchard, went into the barn, and killed Daniel—made a bad movie. The sequel—where she lied that he hadn't brought a body out of the barn, wrapped it in a tarp, and left it in front of the tool shed—should be laughed at.

We went to the tavern for supper. She considered the presence of Daryl, Kathy, the bartender, the server, and half a dozen other customers. Witnesses without an obvious agenda saw them in town. If Linc had had blood on his clothes, at least one person should have noticed. Did one of them lie and say they did? Can they ignore statements of all the others? What did they have? Or think they had? Why all the interest in Linc's work boots?

"Mr. Wayne White, do you believe me?" She wrapped the blanket tight and turned her face to the wall.

Questions continued to chase each other around her mind as she lay quiet, staring at the fine cracks in gray paint over darker gray concrete. How did Daniel Larson die? Who mentioned a beating? Was Basil headed to Hilltop or another place?

"No." She sat up, clinging to the blanket. A tie between Basil and the drug lab shone before her, more distinct than a freeway on a map.

Chapter Seventeen

Linc thumbed through the bills, counted his credit cards, and checked for insurance cards before tucking his wallet into his pocket. He turned to Daryl as he slipped on his watch. "Where's Mona?"

"Her bail didn't arrive with yours." The private investigator continued a text conversation on his phone.

"But …" Linc followed his friend to the outside steps. She deserved to be released. How could they get married with her in jail? "My parents posted mine, right?"

"Put up their house for security. I believe they added a little cash from a retirement fund."

Linc rubbed a day's stubble on his jaw. It sounded right that the house wouldn't be enough; his parents lived in a neighborhood where too many homes had been foreclosed, dragging down all the values. "I expected they would add a little for Mona. They know about the wedding. We Skyped a couple of days ago. Good conversation."

"Not a matter of approval. Let's walk." Daryl led them past a World War I artillery piece posed on a small patch of lawn. He continued across grass to a wooden bench at the foot of the main courthouse entrance.

"She can get out for what, ten percent?" Linc pulled out his phone before sitting down. "Let me check my own accounts. I don't want her there past lunch."

"No need to panic."

"Not for you." Linc visualized his careful plans to claim the farm, plant more acres in orchard, and live with Mona toppling on him like poorly stacked bales. Today was his final chance. Be married by midnight. Or—or Mona would slip away from him. His fingers paused above the screen at the realization he wanted her, wanted to marry her today, or tomorrow. With or without the inheritance. He tapped in his bank password and selected the account he'd reserved for orchard expenses.

Sunshine warmed his face as he fought back panic. What if his balance was a little shy? Mona's image from the courtroom returned. Orange scrubs too large for her petite frame. Her mouth sealed in neutral. A soft gasp as the judge announced the amount of bail. He needed to talk to her. Give her assurance he cared. Get a dose of courage from her amazing deep, dark eyes.

Daryl stood. "Time to walk over and talk to the clerk."

"Does that mean what I think?" Linc aped the investigator's movements.

"It means, my dear young man, that by the time we cross the threshold of the office the transfer should show in the computer. Your parents are taking her bail out of a separate account. Certain financial institutions take a little longer. Even on a Tuesday morning."

Linc picked up his pace, held the door, and took the steps to the office two at a time. Mona would be out of jail and able to marry him.

Twenty minutes later Linc ended his phone call to Pastor Ben Cobb and smiled at Mona.

She frowned and shook her head, as close to ignoring him as possible in the small space where released prisoners reclaimed their personal possessions.

"What?" He closed his mouth before he made a fool of himself in front of three deputies and Daryl. Talk to me. It would be a long, tense trip to Eau Claire if she blamed him for yesterday. He avoided watching her hands as she inventoried her purse.

A minute later she headed for the exit with no more than a crook of one finger toward him.

"Hey." He joined her next to the disabled artillery piece. "This whole thing—I didn't see it coming. Don't blame me. Please."

She remained still for a long moment while a light breeze toyed with her dress, making the large red flowers on the skirt appear to dance. He absorbed the image. A petite figure, with curves in all the right places, begged his arms to surround her waist. A mouth drawn firm and her short dark eyebrows serving as exclamation points declared her off limits at the moment. He wanted to learn every bit of humor and intelligence below the clever packaging. All his hours in jail he'd spent thinking of her on the other side of the wall. Near, yet impossible to see, talk with, or touch. He wanted to do it all. Tease out more details of her life and share his little stories. Their conversations over ice cream in the evenings last week assured him they fit together like parts of a hinge. He wanted her on his team, by his side.

She pushed a strand of fine black hair back into place and looked him square in the face. "You have permission to get me out of your life. I've brought you nothing but expense and now a criminal record."

"Not my plans at all." He reached out, lifted her right hand in both of his, and rubbed it with his thumbs. A warm tingle swept up his arms, crisscrossed his shoulders, and lodged above his heart. "I'm thinking we can make a two o'clock wedding, get the signed certificate back here for Mr. White to file before end of business today, and have a quiet celebration tonight."

"You want to marry trouble?"

"No." He stepped forward, wrapped his arms around her, and brushed a kiss on her forehead. "I want to take Mary Monica 'call me Mona' for a bride. I want you to stay forever."

"Taxi for Eau Claire leaves in five," Daryl announced.

* * *

Mona molded against Linc from her hips to her shoulders. Her head tipped back and her mouth invited his lips for a taste without a conscious command. She sighed across his tongue. Forever? Daryl's voice intruded and she eased away, blinked the world back to focus. "Did I hear you right?"

"I meant every word. I want a second chance to protect you. Keep you close."

"You're not obligated." Her mind raced with possible places to go. Cheap lodging in Eau Claire to comply with the conditions of her release topped the list. Maybe Lorraine would help her find more odd jobs. Then she caught a sparkle from Linc's clear gray eyes. Where had his practical side gone?

"We need to follow Daryl to his car. We've miles to talk."

She gazed at the sky with only enough high thin clouds to relieve the solid blue. It must be the fresh air after the stale, still atmosphere in the jail. Take the risk. She shook her head even as Linc held her hand. One of them needed to remain sensible. Who would believe the story she'd pieced together in the long quiet hours? What if she was wrong and the drugs manufactured by Daniel didn't have a connection to Basil after all?

Linc settled next to her in the back seat, claiming the center seat belt.

She stared out the window, absorbing the sight of scattered businesses and neat farms on their way to the freeway. His arm rested across her shoulders, giving more comfort than any security blanket. Every degree of affection, or imagined fondness, made it difficult to speak of serious matters.

"How much can he hear?" She flicked the hand on her lap toward Daryl.

"Everything." Linc put the word into a smile.

"It won't take me long." She straightened and steadied. "I can be gone and forgotten half an hour after we get to the duplex."

"No."

"It's better that way. Safer."

"I disagree."

It undermined her resolve that he didn't sound disagreeable. She detected warmth and an invitation to share in his voice. She moistened her lips and started again. "I said things ... to the lawyer ... to the detective... that will bring Basil's wrath down on me. And Matt. It might engulf you."

"I'm accused of a murder I didn't commit. How can Basil make it worse?"

"Land is worthless to a dead man." She studied her feet and fought a spasm of nausea.

"I thought he was after your brother."

"He was. He is." She licked her lips and returned her gaze to Linc's face. "He'll find a way."

"I don't see a motive."

"Did they show you photos from the lab in the barn?" She glanced at Daryl and found reassurance in his posture that he paid attention to every word.

"Half a dozen of them. Most were close-ups of things I'd never seen before. Why?" He rubbed the lightest of circles on the back of her hand.

"The molds for the tablets ... that was Basil's design. I wasn't sure at first. So I didn't say anything to the detective. A double B formed into a butterfly is unique to Basil. According to Matt, it's one way he keeps tabs on both dealers and customers."

Linc rested his head against the back of the seat and closed his eyes. "So you think Daniel Larson made the drugs for Basil. It would give him a reason to be in Crystal Springs. Maybe he needed to deliver supplies or pick up product."

"Teach Daniel a lesson. Meet an accomplice." She released the two ideas which had swirled in her head for the last twelve hours.

"The sheriff follows evidence. You're talking like a movie script." Daryl reminded them he followed their conversation while driving.

"I had lots of time to think this over, Mr. Frieberg. Basil has a reputation with his fists. Did the police tell you how Mr. Larson died?"

"Blunt-force trauma. The Whites shared with me." Daryl changed lanes before the freeway exit. "Beaten with a weapon of opportunity—they're looking at shovels and heavy wrenches to find a match. The bar with your prints was too thin for the head wound."

"Can you—" Linc didn't get further.

"I'll kick the investigation in that direction as soon as wedding witness and musician duties are complete."

* * *

Basil caressed the front fender of his El Camino and reviewed the three years spent hunting down parts and restoring the vehicle to showroom condition. Good times, baby. And you're worth every penny. Every minute. "Treat her right, Nick."

"Sure thing. Be careful, boss." The new manager of the warehouse gripped Basil's hand, the fresh star in the cluster on his forearm denoting his promotion.

Basil gave the classic car one more loving, farewell pat and walked over to the dark green minivan. "Open the door, Nick. I'm outta here."

As he eased the van into the street Basil gave his loyal friend a thumbs-up sign. From this moment forward he was out of the drug business. Nick possessed the keys, safe combination, and leads to a new chemist. Basil would never seek out any members of the South Minneapolis organization again. The surrender of his beloved, flashy ride for a blend-into-the-crowd vehicle capable of holding his brother Kevin's wheelchair spoke his exit clearer than words.

Less than five minutes later Basil merged onto the eastbound freeway. One errand, seventy miles to the east, needed to be done before he'd pick up Kevin and drive into the sunset. He felt confident he could convince Mona Smith to cooperate. Her instinct to protect her brother worked in his favor. Plus he carried several photos of Matt enhanced with various injuries to use as incentive to follow his rules. He could picture her a few days from now assisting him with Kevin's care and posing as a loving cousin, or his girlfriend. Yeah, he'd like to feel her small, soft body against him.

I'll pick her up first and convince her later. But he'd have to make it quick, before the police discovered he'd jumped bail.

"First things first." He smiled to the empty passenger seat as he crossed into Wisconsin.

An hour later, Basil parked the van and walked back past one building in the row of duplexes on Benson Place. He adopted the demeanor of a person familiar with the neighborhood and rehearsed a story including concrete repairs. He expected the home to be empty. It was early Tuesday afternoon and Linc worked. Mona appeared to either have a job or a new friend with the woman at the greenhouse. But a stop would be prudent. She might be home. Or left an indication of her location. He wanted to find her quick, and alone.

He pressed the doorbell once, listened to simple chimes, and waited.

Silence. No radio or TV. No footsteps or kitchen appliances. He pulled out his picks and entered the house.

He glanced up the short flight of steps. A glimpse of a recliner convinced him this was the main living level and best place for a clue to Mona's current location. A suit coat on the back of a chair and a red tie tossed across the table seemed at odds with a normal weekday. The great room seating area and open blinds to the small deck seemed normal enough. He stepped into a small room at the top of the steps and found a computer in sleep mode. Papers, magazines, and a few manila envelopes lay scattered across the flat surfaces.

He nudged the mouse with a knuckle. A menu emblazoned with The Bronze Feather over a faded collection of game birds morphed into view. He searched the screen, found an address, and frowned. Why the interest in a supper club outside of Wagoner, Wisconsin? Eau Claire contained nice restaurants without the hour drive on two-lane road. *Not my business.*

A quick walk and inspection of the downstairs rooms didn't tell him what he wanted to know. Mona's backpack sat under a small table decorated with two framed photographs. The bed was made and no stray clothing or notes lay in plain sight. Linc's room appeared on the tidy side without any sign of a woman. *Is there something wrong with the man? Basil would never have an attractive woman in his place this long without installing her in his bed.*

He took the short flight of steps back to the foyer and tested the walk door into the garage. The door swung open and he stood still, afraid to breathe.

Linc's van sat parked on the right side of the garage. White paint and a chrome bumper gleamed in the subdued light. A trace of auto wax confirmed a recent, careful wash.

Where are they? Sweat seeped on his neck. Unexpected. Uncertain. He forced an exhale. He fought the instinct to flee. Better to call on cold logic and explore all of his options. Yes, he'd leave. But not in any sort of a panic.

He returned to the foyer, closed the door, and wiped the hardware clean of any stray prints.

One more peek into the office. His foot touched the second step and froze. A vehicle approached on the small street. He stayed still as a rock and listened. The engine came close, stopped.

Basil glanced out the glass portion of the foyer door, swallowed hard, and sped up the stairs. A moment later he secured the slider to the deck behind him and descended the open wooden steps.

"Don't dawdle." A male voice escaped from the duplex.

"Five minutes. No more."

Mona's voice. Basil remained under the deck and pressed against the wall between the two lower-level windows. A second man spoke indistinguishable words. Water ran from a tap while shoes slapped against hard flooring.

Basil steadied his breathing and estimated his chances of walking to his van undetected. Negative numbers. He pressed his back against the siding and listened to his heart rate level off.

Mona hummed a cheerful tune and adjusted the blinds on the window to his left. He glanced over and relaxed. She'd not see him with a casual look outside.

The footsteps caused him more concern. Who was the second man? He held his breath as the slider moved and a man walked across the deck.

"I'd forgotten what a nice view you have."

"By now I should have the flower boxes out there. But I've been a little distracted."

Basil watched through the narrow slits between the deck boards as the man braced both arms on the rail.

The man laughed before speaking and looking down. "Distracted? When did you become the master of understatement, Lincoln?"

Dray's inside. Who's outside? He molded against the wall without moving.

"Elegant speech fails me at the moment. There. All set. I told Mona I'd wear my red tie to complement her dress."

"Chinese good luck?"

A second serving of cold sweat coated Basil's neck. How much did the man see between the deck boards? A shadow? More? His tattoos itched under the imagined gaze of this stranger.

"Something like that. Are you ready?"

"In a minute. Go ahead. I'll follow. Altoona Road, Chapel of the Pines. Right?"

"Yeah." A dozen silent question marks followed the single word.

"Go. I've a couple of calls to make. I'll lock up."

Trusts this man to let him lock up. He suspected a trap with the address but held it in the front of his memory, just in case. In case of what? A church on Tuesday? Only time he came close to a chapel during the week was to check out a funeral. He waited as the sheen of sweat swelled and merged into rivulets, tracing an irregular path under his shirt. Would the man on the deck follow his bold words with actions? Would he force a confrontation? He could take him in a fair fight. He flexed his hands, confident they could even the score against anything—except a gun.

Basil moved only his gaze as the man above him paced, leaned against the rail, moved a deck chair, and sent text after text on a phone. Five minutes crawled past as he stood in the shade, pressed against the building, sweating.

"Chapel of the Pines on Altoona Road." The man spoke it like an invitation or clue in a scavenger hunt before he re-entered the house and closed the sliding door.

Chapter Eighteen

"I, Mary Monica, do take Lincoln Tyler Dray as my lawful husband, to honor, cherish, and respect as long as we both may live." Mona worked a plain gold ring past Linc's knuckle. She moved her gaze up over black suit, hesitated for an instant on his bright red tie, and hurried up to his face.

He's smiling. She exhaled tension into the small chapel. The room was large enough to hold eighty if they sat close and friendly. Another glance at the ring of silver stars painted on a blue band high on the wall grounded her to time and place. Her grandmother would be astounded that not one statue or painted saint adorned the worship space. A plain wooden cross, polished to a gleam, served as a worship focal point. *It fits this business transaction posing as a wedding.*

Ben Cobb, pastor of Chapel of the Pines, stood in front of that cross now, holding a tiny book in one hand.

She exhaled and looked again at Linc. Perhaps her heart would calm now that her speaking part was over. A tremble swept up her arms as she inspected his face. Gray eyes, straight nose, and generous lips shaped into a small smile combined to kick her heart into a faster pace. She tested a smile and found it easier than expected.

"Having declared themselves before God and this company," Ben Cobb raised his right arm and gestured over the entire attendance of five people, "I now pronounce you husband and wife. You may kiss your bride, Linc."

Promises. Anticipation mixed with memory, propelling her heart loud and fast. Mona sighed into Linc's kiss. The first soft touch simmered for an instant, then burst into full heat. One quick sweep of his tongue across her welcoming mouth later, he eased back. She sealed her lips, savored the trace of salt and mint mouthwash left behind. They're going to hear my heart. I expect it to explode.

"Later. More later." Linc mouthed the words, keeping them private.

She drew back, settled a little, and smiled. She didn't trust her voice. Feeling as light as helium, she clung to his hand before turning to face their witnesses.

Daryl, Lorraine, and Dr. Terrier clapped.

"Well done."

"It's official now."

"Take the rest of the day off." Dr. Terrier grasped the handles of his walker and struggled to stand.

"Come to lunch with us. Our treat," Lorraine added.

"First we need to sign the papers." Ben Cobb reminded them.

A moment later Mona stood at Linc's elbow and watched him sign with a cheap, black stick pen. He started with a large loop in the "L," moved quickly and echoed it with an equally oversize oval on the final "Y." He offered the pen. "Next?"

She skimmed her palms down her skirt to dry them before accepting the ballpoint.

"Mary Monica Smith" in her small combination of printing and cursive looked insignificant beside his confident signature. "Penmanship's not my thing."

"I didn't marry you for your handwriting." He kept his voice pitched soft, between only the two of them.

She stifled a giggle before pushing the document to her right and handing the pen to Daryl. "The only talent I'll claim is cooking."

"Don't underestimate yourself. You're a good driving student. I'll let you move up to the van this weekend."

"Unless we are otherwise engaged." Heat rushed up her neck at the double meaning in her words. She'd intended them to be a light reference to the legal tangle and uncertain future only lawyers and judges controlled. Would he take them as an opportunity to renegotiate the terms of this business arrangement disguised as a marriage?

Linc laughed before brushing her cheek with a thumb. "Careful. We may have to discuss our rules if you keep tempting me."

"Eve with an apple?"

"I prefer to think she used a fig. After all, they needed the leaves soon after."

Mona's laugh escaped past her hand close to her mouth. Life with Linc invited her on an adventure. The days and weeks, even years if she dared to dream, might turn out confusing. But it would not be dull.

"Pardon me for a few." Mona excused herself from the group ten minutes later after signatures and photos on two cameras plus a phone. She followed the pastor's directions to the steps and found the basement ladies' room.

A bride. She spread her hands above the sink and admired the plain gold wedding band. She blinked away a twinge of regret and blotted her face with a paper towel. Her mother would never see her as a bride. Never get acquainted with Linc, a man who managed to show her more kindness and decency in two weeks than all her previous boyfriends combined. Never see grandchildren. Where did that spring from? She checked her makeup and whispered to her mirror image. "Separate bedrooms."

Mona pushed open the door, flicked the light off, and stepped forward.

"Not a word." Basil's voice grated against her ear while one hand pressed against her mouth and the other held an arm behind her back.

* * *

Linc reviewed signatures on the marriage certificate as he slipped the document with a bold, gothic script heading into a plain manila envelope. A memory of the wedding kiss intruded and he almost missed Ben's comment.

"Congratulations and good luck, friend."

"Thanks. I need the luck." Linc noticed a shadow cross a window. "We'll be gone in a few minutes and you can return to your normal life."

"Summer's slow for school bus drivers. Don't have a scheduled run until Friday."

"Sounds a long way from Tuesday." Linc fingered the document envelope and allowed his mind to drift back to Mona. He wanted to give her more than a roof over her head and the occasional kiss for public display. One taste of her, like at the end of the ceremony, compared to resting one drop of ice cream on his tongue. He wanted an entire spoonful. A dish rounded full. An entire pint.

"Outrageous," Lorraine commented with a laugh.

He glanced at the small group clustered around Dr. Terrier and his walker. Did they feel it? The air in the room teased the fine hair on his fingers. He gathered a breath and pushed back analogies with the electric air of thunderstorms. The weather was fine today, mild and partly cloudy. No mass of superheated air to fuel lightning this early afternoon.

Daryl gestured to him as he began to walk to the rear of the chapel.

We need to talk. You explain. I'll listen. In their less than a minute of secluded conversation prior to the ceremony the older man had told him that he'd contacted all the proper authorities. Who did he mean? What had he seen out on the deck to prompt an announcement of their destination?

"Damn." The male voice swept up the stairway clear as a thunderclap.

Daryl doubled his speed and Linc stayed at his heels down the steps.

Where is she? Linc looked around at the empty fellowship area, glanced at Daryl searching the kitchen, and touched the ladies' restroom door before he saw motion outside the frosted windows facing the parking lot.

"This way." Linc motioned to Daryl and sprinted for the exit.

Mona kicked and flailed against a stocky man forcing her toward a green van with the side door open.

"Let her go." Linc ignored a movement to his left and hurried forward.

"Police. Stop."

Linc halted and felt Daryl brush past as a uniformed officer from the Eau Claire County sheriff's department ran into view. An instant later the deputy body slammed Mona's would-be captor and separated them.

Daryl grabbed one arm of the assailant and propelled the man against the van's door.

"Are you—?" Linc assisted Mona to her feet.

"I'm okay."

"Sure?" He skimmed his hands across her shoulders and down her back while studying her face. "Is that—?"

"Basil Berg." She forced the words out between irregular breaths.

Linc stared at the man he'd only seen from a distance at the airport. He stood still, hands behind his back, one cheek pressed against the van. Daryl peered into the open door and the police officer held tight to one wrist.

"Will you be pressing charges?"

"Yes," Linc blurted before Mona opened her mouth. "Assault."

"And stalking," she added.

"Plus attempted kidnapping." Daryl pointed to duct tape, rope, and a shopping bag of women's clothing.

The officer pulled Basil away from the van and recited the Miranda rights as he propelled him toward the cruiser.

"Talk to me, Daryl." Linc massaged Mona's hand, unwilling to break the warm, confused sensation of her touch.

"I apologize for not making time for a more complete explanation. Mona needed to act naturally. I'd already spooked him a bit at the house."

Mona gasped. "The house? Today?"

"While you were downstairs freshening up. Linc never leaves the rod out of the slider track, so I went out on the deck. Viewed his boots through the gaps."

"Why not call the police then?" She clenched Linc's hand painful hard.

Daryl tipped his head toward the officer talking on the patrol car radio. "It's not illegal to be outside your house. So I told him where we were headed and hoped he'd be foolish enough to follow. I also texted a friend with the sheriff's department and requested a surveillance unit."

"Matt. We need to warn Matt. What if—"

"We'll call. In a few minutes." Linc started to guide Mona back inside the building just as Ben, Lorraine, and Dr. Terrier reached the bottom of the handicapped ramp. "You're limping."

Mona reached down and removed her right shoe. When she held it up, the three-inch heel hung by a thin piece of vinyl. "I spiked him. In the shin. I think. After I bit his finger."

"Brave bride." Linc leaned over and brushed his lips against her cheek. "Hey. May I?"

He didn't wait for her verbal response. The instant she stilled he found her lips and pressed against them. She tasted sweeter, more fulfilling, than ice cream. *Let me protect you. Let me love you.*

* * *

Basil stretched out his legs and leaned back in the metal chair. The glass bubble around the surveillance camera shone bright in the corner of the room. Police liked their suspects nervous, so he'd strike a relaxed pose and ignore that turmoil in his stomach. He crossed his ankles and discarded the notion of a smile at the one-way glass. How long to find a lawyer in this burg?

What attracted him to the Smith girl? She was pretty in an exotic sort of way, no question. But he could have asked any of half a dozen of the girls that hung on the edges of the drug gang and found a willing companion. Kevin? Mona Smith would learn quickly how to soothe and care for his brother. Where the other girls would recoil at Kevin's habits, or lack of them, he could imagine her reading to him or helping him use his walker to keep a little strength in his legs.

He'd suspected a trap. Every word he'd heard under the deck this morning pointed to it. And he'd walked right in. He glanced down at his restrained hands and gave a soft laugh. For the first time in a decade he'd crossed the threshold of a church. *You were wrong, Mom. The roof didn't collapse.*

He turned his face toward the door as it creaked open.

"Mr. Berg? I'm Edwin Dolan, public defender."

"Pardon me for not standing." Basil rattled his handcuffs and their attachment to a ring set into the table edge. He scanned the young man in front of him. Mr. Dolan didn't look old enough to shave, let alone be a law school graduate.

"Now, then." The lawyer claimed a seat across the table and opened a slim folder. "It looks bad for an assault charge. We might be able to do something about this attempted kidnapping portion."

"Kidnapping? Is that what the bitch claims?" Basil leaned forward. "You get the camera turned off?"

"Absolutely."

He settled back in his uncomfortable chair. At least the man understood the basics. "What do they have for this kidnapping?"

"They searched your van, found a change of women's clothes in her size, rope, duct tape, Mapquest printouts. Can you claim the clothes belong to someone else? A sister? Girlfriend?"

"Don't have a sister." Basil hooked his thumbs on the table edge. "I want to stay quiet. Make 'refuse to answer' my answer."

"Okay. This is what I expect to happen."

For several minutes Basil and Mr. Dolan talked about procedure. The police were certain to know about the charges in Minneapolis and the judge would deny bail. Extradition to Minnesota could go either way; did Basil have a preference?

During the conversation Basil gained a quiet respect for the young man sitting with his back to the viewing window and blocking most of his own facial expressions from any law enforcement personnel trying to break the lawyer-client privilege rules.

"Can we classify the girl and her friend as unreliable? I hear River County arrested them not long ago."

"That would be a stretch." Mr. Dolan checked his notes. "Another of the witnesses, Mr. Frieberg, is retired Secret Service and a licensed private investigator."

"Damn. He set the trap." Basil rested both forearms on the table and displayed his multi-star tattoo. "Refuse to answer. It's the only reasonable way for me to go. You agreed?"

Mr. Dolan nodded and left the room.

Basil calculated a timeline during his wait. He'd take extradition. Request it, even. At least it would get him away from that private investigator. The more he pondered the man on the deck the more certain he became that he'd seen the man before. Crystal Springs? He needed to get among friends. By tomorrow he'd set in motion events that would make Mona Smith regret even the misdemeanor charges.

A few minutes later Basil inspected the two people following Mr. Dolan into the room. The plainclothes officer wasn't a surprise. Every county employed a detective with varying amounts of experience, and he'd observed the uniformed officer that brought him in speaking to this man before they closed the door to the interview room.

He blinked back surprise at the woman. She wore a chocolate and tan uniform with badges of one of the Wisconsin counties and a no-nonsense expression.

Female officers asked the worst questions and this one carried an air of competence on her shoulders.

Several minutes into the interrogation, the woman, Sheriff Bergstrom, opened the serious questions. "Describe your acquaintance with Mona Smith."

"Not much to tell." Basil gestured to cut off Mr. Dolan's objection. "She's the pretty sister of a work associate. I'd like to know her better."

"Do you threaten all your girlfriends?"

"I don't have to answer that."

"No, you don't." The detective turned to the next report in his folder. "Minneapolis faxed a preliminary report regarding a recent search of Ms. Smith's apartment. Whose prints will they find on the boning knife?"

Basil tensed, dropped his hands below the table, and shifted his feet. What sort of stories had Matt's sister spread? He'd meant the break-in as a warning and she'd taken it seriously enough to scamper away. Two, maybe three, lucky breaks were the only way he'd found her in Eau Claire under the protective eye of Mr. Boy Scout.

"My client doesn't need to answer." Mr. Dolan jotted a note.

"Mr. Berg." The woman spoke in the sort of voice sons obeyed. "Please tell us about your visit to Crystal Springs, Wisconsin, ten days ago. It was a Saturday. Witnesses place you there in the afternoon. Just to refresh your memory."

Basil let his silence stretch long, and signaled his lawyer to remain quiet.

"We have multiple witnesses that put you in the area. Multiple. Reliable." She stared at him in a dare.

Basil twitched his shoulders and stared back.

"Is this one of your business associates?" She slid a glossy color enlargement of Daniel Larson's DMV photo across the table.

He blinked. "I don't have to answer."

"These molds tested positive for traces of high-quality ecstasy." She set another photo on top of the first. "Molds with a monogram matching the tablets found on your person, on several of your associates, and on the premises of your arrest early Saturday morning. One week after you were seen in my jurisdiction. Exactly one week after Daniel Larson, manufacturer of illegal drugs, was murdered."

"I've never killed anyone." Basil's words escaped before he could seal his lips.

"What's your shoe size, Mr. Berg?"

"My ... Why do you need to know?" Basil did a mental scramble. The rain should have destroyed his footprints outside. Had he stepped in a puddle of the spilled liquid in the barn? He'd tried to be careful. Right now he couldn't even be sure which shoes he'd worn. He thought it was the engineer boot with the smooth sole, but he wasn't sure. Or did the sheriff enjoy tossing stuff against the wall until something stuck?

"I'd like a moment with my client."

"What about it, Mr. Berg? Will five minutes with a lawyer solve your problems?"

Basil moistened his lips. "I don't need it. I'm done talking."

"Silence speaks volumes, Mr. Berg. We'll be talking again. Soon."

What did she have? The nervous itch across his tattoo begged for a scratch. Daniel had been long past medical help when he'd found him. The additional kick or two from Basil hadn't made a difference between life and death. The orchard owner did the beating. Daniel's own words in the notebook gave more than enough motivation. Besides, he'd been careful not to leave fingerprints in the barn. The only time he'd even touched Daniel was to check for a pulse. He'd found gloves before he moved the body. Gloves he burned in a fire pit later that night. They couldn't have physical evidence that put him in the barn.

Linc, the orchard owner and man sheltering Mona Smith, was the guilty party, the one who should be under arrest.

Chairs scraped against concrete and he looked up in time to see the two interrogators stand.

You're looking at the wrong man.

Chapter Nineteen

Mona twisted and kicked. The figure in her dream wrapped tighter around her arm. She jerked and screamed. Again and again she flailed out at the shadow, backing away into the unknown.

Plop. "Ow. Oh."

She opened her eyes and lay panting while the dream faded. A round support came into view. A pole? Two blinks later she recognized the futon leg and started to feel a throb in her hip. Stupid nightmare. She sighed. Her legs and arms were tangled in the bed sheet and she started to work one hand around to find the edge.

"Hey." Linc's voice followed two light taps on the door. "You okay in there?"

"Give me a minute." Her fingers hurried and she kicked the bottom of her cotton cocoon loose. "Door's open."

"What? Let me help you." He stood for a moment in the doorway, his face in shadow.

I invited him in? "No, I can do this." She pulled up and sat on the edge of her bed using the tangled sheet like a shield. "Only a dream. Nightmare after a hard day."

"It sounded serious from the other side of the wall."

"Sorry if I woke you." She looked at him and her throat clogged with frozen air. He stood backlit and beautiful. Running shorts, the only clothing he wore, displayed well-shaped muscles on long arms and legs. Previous hints of strength through his regular wear faded. She lowered her gaze and concentrated on straightening the sheet.

"No problem. I wasn't sleeping much." He moved forward, reached past her, and turned on the desk lamp.

She stared at her toes, red polish intact, peeking out. "Do I want to know the time?"

"Four, give or take." He settled on the far end of her bed.

"I'm worried about Matt." She grabbed the first topic to pop into her mind. Anything to keep her from reaching out and wrapping her body around Linc. Her arms ached to hold the real man a hundred times stronger than in the final minutes before she'd fallen asleep.

Linc nodded. "Clarence White called the prison. I don't think we can do more."

"I want to visit him."

"Impossible."

She blew out a long, steady stream of air. Going to see Matt, the only way she'd feel reassured of his health, was forbidden by the terms of her bail. She and Linc were restricted to six of the western Wisconsin counties. The judge, or prosecutor, or both considered the map and permitted them enough geographical space to travel the primary routes from Eau Claire to Wagoner and Crystal Springs. "I know. But—"

"He's your brother. Your family."

"All I have left."

Quiet settled like a welcome guest in the dim light. Mona continued to loosen her binding and checked that her extra-large T-shirt covered all the vital parts before she allowed the sheet to drop to her waist. "I'm sorry I woke you. I'll try not to let it happen again."

"Whoa there. We're in this together. Remember those vows before God and selected witnesses today? Or rather, yesterday."

"We have a business deal masquerading as a marriage." She risked a long, careful look at him. An invitation to move close and rest against his bare chest radiated out, threatened to pull her in like a nail drawn to a magnet. She moved her legs up and wrapped both arms around her knees. "I'm a public wife." A momentary glance away from him allowed her to steady her voice. "And that's okay. We've known each other such a short time."

"Short, but intense." He lifted one end of the sheet from the floor and untwisted a portion. "You ... forced me out of a rut. Gave me ... new experiences?"

"Is that what you're calling a night in jail?" A smile argued with seriousness within her mouth.

"I'm not great with words."

"I've noticed." Mona listened to her heart beating triple loud. Could he hear it? Silence between them occurred often, the vast majority of their quiet moments best described as companionable and easy. This moment nagged at her and sent a mixture of energy and caution to her nerves. They sat on a bed in a dim room. Neither of them wore an abundance of clothes. And—she pressed her lips tight—there was that wedding this afternoon. Yesterday. And Basil. She shivered at the memory of the attempted kidnapping.

"My chances of any more sleep are zero. What about you?"

"Not worth a try." Please leave. She wanted temptation to walk away, take a cold shower, or give her the opportunity for one.

"Tell me about the photos." He pointed to the desk.

"Mother on the left. Granny and Grandpa Chen behind the cracked glass." Relax. He's earned the right to ask about family. She busied her hand with the sheet, welcomed an excuse not to look at him. Too much inviting skin.

"Nice." He went to the desk and picked up her mother's picture. "What was her name?"

"Christine."

He whispered the full name, Christine Chen Smith, twice before setting the photo down. "You've mentioned your grandmother. Why not grandpa?"

"I barely remember him. He died a long time ago." She stared at the crack in the glass that gave an appearance of a scar across the man's neck. Anger at the scene in her apartment bubbled and threatened to erupt. She willed a happier memory forward: sitting on his lap, holding her yellow rabbit, and learning math in Cantonese. "The year I turned five."

"It's hard to remember five. Did you go to kindergarten?"

"Couldn't understand why Matt didn't go with me. We'd been inseparable." She hooked wayward hair behind an ear. "He's fourteen months younger. I think I've been looking out for him since he started to walk. And get in trouble."

He squatted in front of her. "Hey. A dependable older sister is good for a boy. Madison saved me time-outs and swats on the behind any number of times." He lifted her chin with one finger until they their eyes aligned. "No apologies for nightmares. Got it?"

She blinked understanding and permitted her lips to curve into a smile. If he held his finger against her skin for another ten seconds she'd not be responsible for her arms wrapping around him.

"I'll dress for a run and be back in half an hour."

"Good." She pushed her open fingers through her hair. "I mean, that's fine. You haven't been able to run." Her mouth refused to form sensible words with all the pheromones colliding in the air. "I'll have the coffee ready when you return."

"Hey. This snarl in our life will be long forgotten in a hundred years."

Her laugh refused to be held back. An arrest, night in jail, wedding, and assault demanded more attention than tangled string. He put too much confidence in lawyers and the justice system. Perhaps she did the opposite. "Go. Run. Today we've work to do."

Five minutes later Mona stepped into the shower and turned on a blast of cold water. She soaped, shampooed, and rinsed while her thoughts attempted to organize the different slices of her life.

The career girl insisted on first place. She itched for a return to restaurant work and school. In good moments she'd imagine framed diplomas on an office wall, impressing new hires and salesmen. It would be her place. Either as franchise owner or an independent café—Mona Smith's dream come true.

Matt's image drifted into her thoughts and reminded her of family obligations. He didn't deserve his current sentence. And he needed protection from the remnants of Basil's organization. Yes, Matt earned the title of thief. He was guilty of several instances of burglary and many other sins. She refused to believe he'd assaulted the elderly homeowner, the charge that sent him from county jail to state prison. How could she help remove the darkest layer of grime from him? Certainly not with a high-priced lawyer. Debt from their mother's final, short illness threatened to gobble her income and small, positive credit rating.

Linc's wife. The role would challenge a drama major. Starting today, with Lorraine, she'd smile, avoid direct comment on the wedding night, and pretend to be in love with him. She'd be dutiful and move to the farm when all the inheritance dust settled. Out of necessity, she'd learn to drive. The list of things to do and learn looked endless from this vantage point. Find a job with an easy commute. Enroll in the nearest restaurant management program and deal with transferring credits. Learn more about growing and selling apples in addition to cooking them.

No apologies for nightmares. How much of this morning had been an act? His appearance in her room soothed her nerves after the dream and embarrassing fall out of bed. In the light of day he could be, already was, a friend. And the rest of the time?

She wrapped a towel around her body and headed back to her bedroom. Assembling a life out of this mess would be more complicated than a thousand-piece puzzle without the aid of the picture on the box. Not even a descriptive paragraph to aid her.

She addressed the family photos as she shook out her last clean shirt. "Any proverbs for me, Granny Chen?"

* * *

Too close. Linc jogged up a long slope and focused on the parking lot at the top. He ran toward the east, where the sky started to show a faded gray ahead of actual sunrise.

Slap. Slap. Slap. His running shoes hit against asphalt in a steady rhythm. He listened and shook his head. Not enough runs. Out of routine. He pushed forward and counted on one hand the number of morning exercise sessions since Mona ran into his life. A few paces later he turned into the parking lot and paused long enough to do a few resistance stretches against a light pole.

"Business agreement. Public marriage." Did she have any idea how close to the edge this morning took me? Mona, rumpled, tangled, and lost in a faded shirt matched the appeal of the shorts, jeans, or swirl of her dress. Wedding dress. He smiled as the image of Mona holding the damaged shoe after her tussle with Basil surfaced.

What had Daryl called her before he left the police station yesterday? Charming dynamo? Well, he'd agree with the charm in a blink. Her lips, her eyes, came within a leaf's thickness of undoing all his calm, rational words of the past two weeks the instant he touched her chin this morning. The memory of it heated his lips. *Why didn't I kiss her? Pick her up and carry her to my bed?*

If I ever find out you forced a woman you'll answer to the both of us. His dad's voice circled in warning mode. Linc trotted along the path leading toward home—and temptation.

Each breath along the rest of his run included a little determination to do this right. Stand by his legal wife. Support without smothering. And don't touch in private. His shoulders sagged under the weight of it.

"Coffee smells delicious," he called from the foyer before closing the door behind him.

"It's just getting started." Mona's voice beckoned him like water attracts roots during a drought.

He hesitated on the bottom step. No, he'd already argued that topic, less than a minute ago. "I'll be up after a shower."

"Sounds good."

Her voice echoed in Linc's brain as he hurried through a shower and shave. As he pulled on clean work clothes he remembered her face when he'd first turned on the lamp in her room. *What did she imagine I slept in?* In an instant his mind put new sleepwear over her petite, athletic frame. *Near nothing. I'd like short and sheer. And red. For good luck.*

Mona stood at the stove and tipped scrambled egg mixture into the pan. "Was it a good run today?"

"Overdue. I've missed too many in the past couple of weeks." *Since you swept into my life with your plea to pretend.* "Tulips at the dental clinic are over. Lilacs are especially good this year."

"Flowers again. I'm not used to your references yet."

"I figured I'd go in a little early today. Might be a good day to catch up on the greenhouse things before I start the client route."

"Lorraine won't need me at the Polk Street house until nine. I'll take the bus. Save you the bother of taking me."

"It's not a bother." He'd enjoy her company as he organized pots and mixed plant food. He poured juice for two and risked a careful look at her eyes. The physical, lustful portion of him awakened again. He glanced away before he did something reckless, like pull her away from the stove and carry her down to his bed until noon—tomorrow. "Have you figured out the buses already? You only got the pass Friday."

"And I intend to use it. I checked the website and made a few notes. I'll be fine. I've been getting on the bus by myself since first grade."

"Not here."

She released a little musical laugh and tended the eggs. "You worry too much."

"You're my wife. I think it's in the job description."

"I don't remember 'worry' as part of the vows."

He added napkins to the holder between their place settings and searched his memory for the exact words they'd decided to include. "It's implied. Invisible glue between honor and cherish."

"Drink more coffee. You're not awake if you think worry is glue."

"I'll call you around noon, when I get a break between clients." He waited for her to settle in her chair before he dug into his eggs. "How many days before the estate sale?"

Mona chewed and swallowed a bite of toast. "Three, counting today. The auction company will come in on Friday afternoon and take over."

"And Saturday? Do you need to be there?"

"I doubt it. I've been the unskilled labor. I don't know much about the value of the dishes and furnishings." She traced an index finger along the mug handle. "I might walk into it all done today. I've been gone long enough."

"You look skilled to me. I need to spend Saturday at the orchard. Will you come? We'll have access to the bathroom in the house." He sipped coffee.

"Tempting me with indoor plumbing?"

He grinned. "I called the Larsons and they don't mind, even promised to move Daniel's things out by the end of the month."

"You went to a lot of effort if you called Daniel's family. Considering the arrest and everything, I'm surprised they spoke to you."

"I'd really like your company." He glanced into the bottom of his mug while he organized his thoughts. How do you explain relationships of a lifetime in a sentence or two? "Joe Larson, his wife, and the rest of the family are decent people. I've never quarreled with any except Daniel."

"How many of the locals know about the arrest?"

"All of them." He walked to the coffee maker and returned with the carafe. "Instant communication is a hallmark of small towns like Crystal Springs. It's as fast as the Internet and about as accurate."

"Then maybe we should put in an appearance at the local tavern. I don't want it rumored that you married a two-headed crone for money."

Chapter Twenty

Mona set the last of the empty gas cans in the van and walked toward the farm house. Twilight masked the flaws Linc pointed out during an introduction earlier in the day. The need for a new coat of paint and the mismatch of shingles where emergency repairs had been made blended into shadows. It's a grand house. With two stories, two full baths, and four bedrooms it was larger than anything she'd lived in. Even the place they rented years ago, when her dad lived with them—three small bedrooms, one bath, and a screened porch—paled aside this one.

Will I ever live in it? She swallowed hard, trying again to banish the fear that the county prosecutor would continue with the murder charges. In the daylight she realized that Daryl Frieberg and Clarence White had asked questions and looked in all the right places to find evidence to clear them. Then every night visions of jail and separation from Linc intruded. By morning her pillowcase wore a damp spot from tears. So far she'd not been able to decide if she cried for Linc, Matt, or herself.

"What are you thinking?" Linc walked up to within an arm's length.

Touch me. Come closer and hold me. She held in a sigh and resisted the magnetic pull to initiate touch. All day, since he prepared bacon and pancakes for Saturday breakfast until this minute, she'd made a conscious effort to limit contact to a few touches of their hands. She ached for the affection in his touch at the same time she feared it. She laced her fingers, risked a glance at her ring, and then looked at the back steps. "I'm admiring the house. How old is it?"

"The core was built in the nineteen twenties. My grandparents hired the last major remodel in the seventies."

"It's a lot of house for two people."

"We could rent out rooms. Or fill them with children."

She backed away a step. Children? In a business arrangement? With felony charges dangling in the air? "You're forgetting something."

"Maybe." He closed the distance between them in one easy move before reaching out to caress her cheek. "We can always renegotiate the terms of our marriage. After ..." He brushed his thumb along her jaw soft as new grass. "If you want."

If I want. She sealed her lips. If she spoke from her heart at a time like this, when her body longed for him, which added up to twenty-three hours plus every day, disaster would follow. She looked down at the grass-stained toes of her sneakers in an attempt to blot out the recurring image of a near naked Linc at her bedroom door. "We have time. Didn't Mr. White say the repeat title search and other paperwork would take several weeks?"

"He did."

She sighed before reaching up and caging his wrist with one hand. Millimeter by millimeter she brought his hand close and kissed the palm. Smooth and firm with a trace of salt, she filed the sensation next to their few kisses. She raised her gaze to his eyes and stared for a long moment. "Are you afraid of me?"

He shook his head. "Me. Once I started I don't think I could stop."

"I've never seen myself as a temptress." She lowered their hands and released him. This man, her husband, stirred her emotions at blender puree speed. In rational moments she viewed him as a new acquaintance, a friend who responded well to questions of orchards or his family. All it took was his touch on her arm, or a look across a small space, to stir her hormones like a whisk going through eggs. Her body wanted him close. Her common sense told her to resist him. Their fairy tale would vanish like the stray white clouds decorating the sky. Too many complications littered her life. Paying medical bills and getting justice for Matt should matter more than whether Linc found her attractive enough for another kiss.

"You need a new mirror." He turned toward the van. "Come on, I think Jack's got a pizza waiting for us."

Fifteen minutes later, Mona scanned the tavern patrons as the server walked away with their order. "Not as busy tonight. Not like last time."

Linc sat stiff, with an expression of uncertainty. "I think a crowd is up the street. Daryl mentioned he'd be playing at a wedding today. Legion Hall's popular for the reception."

She nodded while rubbing her arms. The atmosphere was chill, and not from the air conditioner humming in the background. Not one person nodded or spoke a word of greeting to Linc when they walked in. The bartender watched them with a strict professional eye. Is this Crystal Springs shunning?

"Maybe I'm disappointing the locals by not wearing prison orange."

"Hey." He reached across the table and trapped her hand under his larger one. "Where's your courage? Did you leave it on the bus to Polk Street?"

"I'd rather plead sleep-deprived." Did he have the mirror image of her problem each night: lying for what seemed like hours in the dark, listening for a whisper of invitation from the other side of wall? How many nights in a row had she drifted off with images in her mind of Linc sprawled across his bed? She broke their physical connection as the server set down two large mugs of root beer.

"To us?" He lifted his mug toward her.

"To an adventure in rural living?" Her first swallow of cool, sweet root beer took long enough for her to make a decision. I'll act. Let the locals draw their own conclusions. By the time she centered her mug on the cardboard coaster her small smile became genuine.

"I've an idea for your next driving lesson."

"Shouldn't I get a permit first?" She hid a hand on her lap and clenched the fingers at the memory of her terrible minutes behind the wheel of the van today. At least on the tractor her main worry was the portion of the vehicle in front, not behind, the driver's seat.

Linc shrugged. "Technicality you'll take care of before next weekend."

He's more confident in my ability than I am. "Question for you. Why did you count and name insects this afternoon?"

"The ones in my trap?" He waited for her to nod. "Need to know when to spray. And for which pests. I'd like to think I'm a responsible orchardist. Chemicals are necessary for a consistent, even crop. But then again," he said, and leaned toward her, "it would be a waste of time and money, plus bad for the environment, to spray poison for a problem that wasn't present. Make sense?"

"When you put it that way." Mona moved her mug and smiled at both the server and the pizza. She managed to identify three spices but paused as something unexpected blended in. Fennel? "Smells delicious."

"Jack makes his own sauce. Refuses to give out the recipe." Linc teased out the first wedge and maneuvered it to a plate.

"You've asked?"

He handed her the full plate and slid out another piece. "No. My pizza starts frozen. Kathy asks for his recipe every few months."

"So my position as cook is secure?" She followed the first burning bite of supper with a swallow of root beer.

"Definitely."

Mona hid her mouth behind her mug as Corey Maxwell entered and strode toward the bar. Is he sober? Will he make a scene? She forced down another bite of pizza.

"Good to see you, neighbor." Corey grasped a beer in one hand and clapped Linc's shoulder with the other.

Linc glanced up and swallowed in a hurry. "Same. Do you remember Mona?"

"Somewhat. You are a pretty little thing." Corey downed a quarter of his drink. "Came over to offer an apology. Afraid I made a bad first impression the other day. Do that sometimes. When the alcohol gets ahold of me."

"Are you feeling better, Mr. Maxwell?"

"Much. Name's Corey."

She pulled off a section of crust and debated inviting him to join them. "Have you talked to your wife? Patti?"

"Couple of times. When I was sober. Matter of fact, the two of us managed a decent phone conversation just this morning." Corey continued rattling on about the call for another full minute with pauses only long enough for one-word responses. Then without warning he announced that his dog was pregnant and they were welcome to a puppy when the time was right.

"I'll think on the dog offer." Linc gestured to the remaining half pizza. "Have you eaten?"

"Don't want to interrupt anything."

"You won't." Mona handed him one of her extra napkins to use as a plate. She was still digesting the change in Corey from quiet but flirty drunk to chatterbox when he broached a new subject.

"Do you think you'll be keeping that generator in the barn?" Corey moved pizza while aiming the question at Linc.

"Didn't know about one. Joe Larson might have a claim on it."

"Sheriff still has the tape across the barn doors," Mona observed.

"That so?" Corey signaled the server for another round of drinks.

Linc hesitated as if hunting down the right words. "Did you visit Daniel in the lab often?"

"Couple of times." Corey took a big bite and chewed with a smile. "Mmmm. Triple meat and secret sauce. Nothing finer with Leinnies."

"Tell me about this generator. How did he vent it?"

"Big old hose, size of a dryer vent, out the window. Snaked out there six feet or more. Kept the top door open, too. And you know old barns. They leak air up, down, and sideways." He snatched his drink up and saluted Linc. "Safe. Daniel was strict about certain things. Person would have thought he did serious research the way he kept all the equipment clean and wrote down all his results. Now they say he was supplying street drugs to a gang up in the Cities. Generator ran noisy. I'm thinking it might come in handy if we have an ice storm. Keep my well and a little heat going."

Mona clasped her hands in her lap. It didn't sound a bit safe to her.

"Startled poor Daniel out of his wits once when I walked in and he was writing in that notebook of his."

"He kept a record book?" Mona tipped her head in doubt. What sort of criminal, and certainly a chemist manufacturing illegal drugs qualified, kept written records?

"Yes, ma'am. Always at the end of his main work table."

"What did he write?" Linc sipped from his second drink.

"Not sure. Saw numbers and chemical formula stuff once. Last time I walked in he was writing a paragraph of something or other."

She leaned into Corey's space. In all of the photos both the detective and lawyer displayed to her, no sort of binder or pad appeared. "Describe the book."

"It wasn't fancy." Corey looked at her and got thoughtful. "Speckled cover. My daughter used one like it in science class. Recorded her experiments. Teacher insisted it be a bound book. Why?"

Mona eased back as Corey breathed beer fumes in her direction. "I'm just trying to understand the late Daniel Larson. I'm thinking he took his science seriously."

Chapter Twenty-One

Mona's stomach churned in time to the ceiling fans above her. What did it mean—an additional hearing—new information? She shifted on the spectator bench and studied the prosecutor stacking files on his table beyond the aged wood rail. She rubbed at gooseflesh on her arms at the realization of the power the one ordinary man represented for her and Linc.

"Hey," Linc whispered and touched her hand. "We're in this together."

She nodded and lifted her gaze to his eyes. At the moment they showed him as friendly, kind, and concerned about their fates. Before she could speak a word the side door opened and the first defendant was escorted into the courtroom. Basil. She swallowed back the lump of surprise. The assault charges were filed in a different county. Could the man's non-stick coating be wearing thin?

Bright yellow prison scrubs with Hennepin Co. stenciled across the back and shackles on wrists and ankles replaced Basil's usual dark clothing and arrogant stance. He glanced in Mona's direction without a trace of his previous smug expression.

Stay calm. He can't hurt me here. A tingle of cold fear for Matt traveled across her neck. Could he—would he—had he ordered more harm to her brother?

Linc's touch on her arm moved her attention to the second prisoner, now taking a seat in the jury area.

They've arrested Corey Maxwell. Did he brag about trespassing at the crime scene? Or is this something more? Mona held her gaze on him as their farm neighbor rested arms on thighs for only a moment and then moved his fingers in small, restless circles.

"Did you have something to do with this?" She leaned toward Linc.

"A word to Daryl," he replied. "I didn't know what would come of it."

She crossed her fingers for good luck.

"Good afternoon." Clarence White eased next to Linc.

An instant later the bailiff called the court into session and everyone stood.

Mona leaned forward and listened carefully to catch the quiet exchange between Basil, his lawyer, and the prosecutor when they gathered in front of the judge's bench.

"For the charge of second-degree reckless homicide, how do you plead?"

"Not guilty," Basil's lawyer spoke for him.

Three more charges followed. Mona heard enough of the subdued exchanges to understand they related to tampering with a crime scene and destroying evidence. Again Basil pled "not guilty" through his attorney. Then they volleyed bail and conditions. In the end, Basil was denied bail and ended up in custody of Hennepin County, Minnesota pending his next court appearance in River County, Wisconsin.

Mona studied her clenched hands and conquered the urge to bolt from the room before Basil made eye contact. He caused this mess. How many innocent people has he gotten arrested?

"Maxwell versus the State of Wisconsin." The clerk announced the next case, complete with the numbers defining jurisdiction and other details understood only by lawyers.

"Fool." Mr. White muttered as Corey Maxwell and the prosecutor took their places before the judge. "Where's his attorney?"

"Do you have legal representation, Mr. Maxwell?" The judge leaned forward with a pen in his hand.

"No, Your Honor. Not at this time."

Mona turned her attention to Mr. White. He held up three fingers and mumbled. She caught the words "Maxwell" and "conflict of interest."

"I plead not guilty to all charges, your honor." Corey looked straight ahead and ran all the words together.

"The court accepts your plea, Mr. Maxwell." The judge waved one finger at the prosecutor as if reminding him to stay silent. "You are remanded to the county jail until such time as you retain or are assigned legal services. Next case."

Mona tapped Linc's wrist and whispered. "The tavern conversation?"

"The generator, local rumors, and … later." He nodded as the clerk stood to read the next case number.

Mona held her chin high and focused on the national flag behind the judge as she crossed the courtroom. The gentle, steady footsteps of Linc and

Mr. White followed until they stood in a tidy row with the prosecutor in front of the elevated desk.

"Your Honor," the prosecutor began. "In the interest of justice and in light of new evidence brought to the attention of my office, the state requests all charges in the cases of Mary Smith and Lincoln Dray be dismissed."

Mona dared not to breathe. What if the spell shattered? She half expected a television drama director to call out a command.

"Defense concurs." Mr. White spoke clearly, projecting his voice for any spectator to understand without straining.

New evidence. A rumor? Mona remained still and focused on the judge's face as he spoke the formalities of dropping the charges and a final word about collecting their bail. She sealed her lips as a bubble and shout of joy threatened to burst out as the judge tapped his gavel.

"We can go." Linc's voice in her ear and a nudge on her shoulder propelled her into motion.

* * *

Linc paused two steps beyond the courthouse door and tugged Mona beside him, toward a concrete urn filled with bright petunias. "Do you smell it?"

"What?" She paused beside him and took a deep breath. "I feel a summer day. Warm air with a tinge of diesel."

He glanced at an eighteen-wheeler belching a complaint as the driver shifted. "More than that. Freedom. The ugly foreboding when we walked in earlier this afternoon is gone."

"You didn't act afraid in there." She jerked her thumb back to the building.

He controlled the laughter knocking in his throat to a smile. "All my stoic Northern European ancestors come in handy on occasion."

"I have questions. About what happened in there."

"So do I." *More than you can imagine.* He led her over to the planter, studied the sky for an instant, and then buried his face in the colorful, fragrant flowers.

"Watch for the bees."

He straightened, hesitated a heartbeat, and grinned. Did she have a clue how badly he wanted to kiss her? A trace of lipstick remaining from early in the day begged to be tasted. He faced her and rested her elbows in his palms. "Mrs. Dray. I need to get used to saying your name."

"My name's Mona."

He laughed and delayed his urge for more with a light kiss on her forehead. "Come on. Let's go reclaim my parents' mortgage and retirement before the lawyers can calculate their fee."

"The dismissal." She hurried beside him. "Does this mean I ... we ... can visit Matt?"

"Don't see why not. The travel restriction should be lifted."

"They ... the prison officials ... might need to clear you."

"Wouldn't be the first background check I've survived." He kept his voice casual while his lungs tensed. *Do false arrests show? Would even the dismissed charges prevent Mona from seeing her* brother? He struggled against a frown and found one of those ancestral stoic sets for his mouth. He couldn't bear sadness invading Mona's eyes at the moment. This was a time for joy, celebration as a great invisible weight remained on the courtroom floor behind them. He wanted the hope of a moment ago to remain.

All through the paperwork in the clerk's office he battled a dry, tense throat. Until the clerk countersigned and stamped the receipt he feared the judge or prosecutor would call and negate the hearing. Could they do that? He added another question for Jackson to a small mountain. He and his brother needed to have a long, technical conversation during the approaching Fourth of July family gathering.

"Ready for the next stop?" Linc held the door for Mona.

"And that would be?"

"More lawyers. Wayne White said he had papers ready. And I've a couple of questions that shouldn't wait. Especially if we plan a visit to Minneapolis."

A few minutes later the receptionist at White and White announced them as Lincoln Dray and Mona Smith.

Linc sighed. He longed to hear the phrase "Mr. and Mrs." He wanted to protect her. His heart desired to give her all that he possessed, including his name. Would she accept it? Or was she going to stay polite and kind? Would he be filing for a quiet divorce next year after his claim and title to the land stood clear and certain?

"Come on back." Wayne White smiled at them from the hall entrance.

"Ladies first." Linc fell into step at the rear of the small parade. Questions about all the soft words they'd missed in the courtroom grew in importance with each step toward the rear office.

"Now, then." Clarence White settled into his leather chair after brief greetings. "We've got twenty minutes before my daughter-in-law expects to see us walk in her door. What's the first question?"

"What are the exact charges against Mr. Berg and Mr. Maxwell?" Linc's words darted into the air.

"Expected that question." Wayne handed a printed list across the desk. "This is not to leave the office."

Linc scanned down the collection of legal phrases. "Conspiracy? Accessory? Trespassing? Homicide? So they were in it together?"

"That's difficult to prove. Primary theory of the moment claims Mr. Maxwell sought out Daniel Larson and beat him with his fists and weapons of opportunity."

"And Basil ... Mr. Berg?" Mona accepted the list.

"Discovered the victim either dead or dying. Instead of reporting the crime he decided to frame Linc, based on notes available in the barn. He also removed the laboratory notebook, with formulas, procedures, and financial records." Wayne paused. "And all the drugs he found lying around."

"What turned the sheriff in the right direction?" Linc glanced down at his feet and wondered for an instant when or if they would release his work boots from evidence.

"Your friend, Mr. Frieberg." Clarence tapped one finger on the desk. "He visited Patti Maxwell and convinced her to talk to the police. She gave them enough information to support her husband's motive and opportunity."

"And they discovered their physical evidence wasn't as strong as it appeared." Wayne leaned back. "The wear patterns on the boot prints were only close, not exact. And the only tool with Ms. Smith's prints didn't match any wounds."

"Then the rumors of Patti's affair with Daniel were true?"

Both lawyers nodded before Wayne resumed the narrative. "Mr. Berg employed Daniel Larson as his chemist. It wasn't the most congenial of relationships. Anecdotal evidence suggests Mr. Larson displayed a knack for antagonizing people."

"He did. Last time we spoke he mixed general insults with threats to buy the farm and destroy the orchard." Linc glanced down and confirmed the tremble in his hands caused by the mere words and image of Daniel standing defiant at Farm Service.

"Well, case closed. That piece of business, at any rate." Wayne picked up a multiple copy-form and slid it toward Linc. "This is the intent to claim the property. Think of it as the earnest money papers if you were doing a purchase. Sign it today and I'll get the title search started. They'll be a formal session similar to signing closing papers. Would mid-July work for you?"

Linc nodded. He picked up the offered pen and scrawled his name firm enough to make four copies. "Mona. There's a space for you to sign."

Chapter Twenty-Two

"What are you looking for?" Mona gave a final swipe of her cloth across the counter separating kitchen from dining area. Morning and early afternoon events continued to chase each other around in her mind. If pressed, she'd say they'd picked up the pace since their late supper. This morning contained a job interview. The afternoon overflowed with both tension and relief at the hearing and lawyer's office.

She started another review of the mental list, things to do in the near future. A visit to Matt occupied the top spot. And maybe that day trip could expand to retrieve additional clothing and her bicycle from the apartment. Tomorrow she interviewed with Lorraine's friend for a housecleaning job. She needed to look into the Wisconsin technical schools with culinary programs. And—and accept her decision to live with Linc as public wife and private housekeeper.

"Found it." Linc held up the log starter. "Want to join me on the deck? I'm going to light all the citronella candles. My plan is to last more than a minute without making a blood donation."

She rinsed and twisted the cleaning rag. Several bites from two nights ago itched at the casual reference to mosquitoes, the most plentiful wildlife in America's lake-filled upper Midwest. "It's going to be dark soon."

"So? We're adults, able to set our own schedules. I'll still go to work in the morning. And you ... don't you have an interview?"

"Ten thirty with Lorraine's friend."

"Got your bus figured out?"

"Absolutely. She lives three doors away from the Polk Street house."

"Come outside and talk with me." He rested the back of one hand on the counter and curved his fingers in invitation.

"Sounds ominous."

"Don't mean to."

She roamed her gaze over him. He wore ragged denim shorts and a faded blue T-shirt tight enough to hint at his fine-muscled chest. Her heart skipped one beat at the memory of Linc shirtless in her doorway. How long ago was that? Five? Six days. And nights. She closed a mental door on the image that returned every night before exhausted sleep claimed her. "Give me another minute or two in here."

She paused in her task of putting a few dishes away and admired him a moment later. He leaned over and lit a row of scented candles in metal containers. She blinked in surprise as he turned to the small table and touched the flame to the wick of a new candle in bright red glass.

A few moments later Mona closed the screen slider behind her and savored the view. Linc stood with his back to the house, both arms braced on the wooden rail and face tipped to the sky. "The stars will be out soon."

"That's what I'm watching for. My lucky star." He glanced at her, eased off the rail, and wrapped on arm around her waist. "Did you wish on stars when you were a kid?"

"Too much city light." Eau Claire produced distraction with street lighting at something less than half Minneapolis. Stargazing translated to admiring the celebrities on magazine covers in her crowd of friends. "On the farm ... did you learn your stars there?"

"Some. More during the astronomy unit in physics."

"Planetarium visit?" Outdoor scents of cut grass, juniper shrubs, and the candles underlined this view as real life, not a school field trip. She pretended the shiver on her skin came from a puff of breeze and not the touch of Linc's arm against her. Wishes, either on stars or birthday candles, didn't come true for her. If they had ... She banished the fanciful line of thought.

"There it is." He pointed to about one o'clock in the sky. "Want to wish with me?"

She directed her gaze to the spot of light. What could she lose? Her new friends would help her keep a roof over her head at the very least. She closed her eyes tight. *I wish one night of real marriage.*

"Do we have to share?" She broke the silence after she thought her heart would have the neighbors reporting a wandering drummer.

"Forbidden to share. Required to act." He leaned down and brushed his lips across her cheek.

She tipped her head down and held back her next breath. The heat of a blush burned her cheeks.

"Beautiful." He whispered in a kiss behind her ear. "Tempting. You seduce me."

She moved under delicate pressure from one strong finger guiding her chin. *He gives me too much credit. More power than I deserve.* Up. A little to one side. When she lifted her gaze his lips filled the view for an instant before descending to meld with hers.

Mona allowed her mouth to open, sigh against his lips, and beg for more. She wanted this to last forever. She rose to her toes and circled her arms around his neck. One magic moment. One night of dreams come true. Please.

He pulled away, leaving her mouth cold and orphaned.

"Mona." He touched his forehead to hers. "I … we … I want you. If you're willing."

"Let me kiss you." She needed to test if the magic went both ways. One gentle ounce of pressure brought his head down half an inch and she pressed her lips against his mouth. She swept her tongue across his lower lip, exploring and tempting. It felt perfect, heating her desire and cooling impulse at the same instant.

He groaned against her lips. She responded by sliding her tongue deeper into warm secrets. She savored the taste of him, including the trace of mint toothpaste.

"We …" He changed the kiss to chaste. "Sit with me. On the lounge. On my lap."

"To talk?"

"A little." He backed up two steps, settled on the cushion, and tugged her wrists in invitation.

She leaned against him, listening to his heart and resting one arm across the back of his neck. Safe.

"I want you." He sighed into her hair. "Since … oh … I can't put a time to it."

"Our first kiss." She lifted his hand from her lap and circled her thumb across smooth skin. "Do you remember in the kitchen at the Polk Street house? It felt special from my side of things. Different. Tucked full of promise."

"I'll never forget it." He guided her face up and stared into her eyes. I remember the first time I saw you. You intrigued me. I think I got lost in your eyes before we left the airport."

She blinked in slow motion. Did he realize what a compliment he'd given? He was the first, the only man of any personal acquaintance, who didn't lapse into offensive remarks tying her eyes to her Chinese ancestry. She started to form a simple "thank you" but before it could cross her lips he claimed her mouth again. Even simple manners vanished.

Mona didn't attempt to keep track of the kisses, caresses, and sweet nothings they exchanged after that. Want, need, love, and lust all tumbled together in the evening air surrounding them. She dimly remembered extinguishing the candles.

Only one moment outside of the house seared into her mind later. After he opened the slider, she paused in the open door and found Linc's lucky star, their star, shining bright in the cloudless sky.

Coming soon:
Seed of Desire
A Crystal Springs Romance

Chapter One

Beth Cosgrove smoothed the fine hairs on the back of her neck with one hand. Her personal warning system tingled as if a thunderstorm lurked over the horizon. Glancing up, she confirmed the early August sky was clear. No hint of impending danger from Midwest weather. Nothing obviously wrong in the scene around her either. The sights, sounds, and smells reflected the normal controlled chaos of the Annual 4-H Dog Obedience and Agility Trials.

She turned from her view of the judging ring in time to watch a sheriff's department patrol car ease down the fairgrounds main road. It pulled to the side, and the deputy got out to direct traffic. Continuing to turn her head, she checked on the tweens and their dogs under her temporary care.

Four youngsters wearing matching white-and-green club T-shirts sat on the grass near her blue ice chest. Near them, three dogs relaxed on slack leashes in the late morning sun. The fourth dog, a beagle, pawed at the tight turf of the fairgrounds racetrack infield, acting typical for his breed. She smiled as a fifth child approached with a young gray German shepherd by her side.

"Is it time?" the tween asked.

"Almost. The Border collie is on the final figure. Then the judge will give everyone on the far side of the temporary ring a moment before he calls your group." Beth flicked her gaze to the judge on the set up on the racetrack. Easy on the eyes.

The quick observation had her estimating the man near her age of twenty-eight, six foot, and lean. His wheaten hair could use a trim, but she'd forgive him for neglecting the barber shop. It should be illegal for a man to look that good in a white dress shirt open at the neck, the sleeves rolled to the elbow under his green official 4-H judge's vest. Stop it. Men are off-limits.

"Ms. Cosgrove?" The girl rubbed one hand on her denim shorts. "I'm nervous."

"You'll do fine, Amber. Pretend it's a practice session, and Tango will follow your lead."

At the sound of her name, the shepherd swung her head and looked up at Beth.

She shifted her attention to the dog. It wasn't right for a project leader to have favorites. Yet it was difficult not to favor Tango, a daughter of her kennel, part of the most recent litter from Dancer, her first and favorite breeding bitch. At nine months, still classed as a puppy, the animal oozed with intelligence and potential.

"It's going to be exactly like our practice sessions," Beth added.

Metal clanged against metal, making Beth flinch. One quick glance confirmed the noise came from the traveling carnival. They were setting up across the road from the back of the grandstand and would be ready when the River County Wisconsin Fair officially started at noon tomorrow. Within twenty-four hours, the fairgrounds would be a whirlwind of activity, with exhibitors putting the finishing touches on displays and performing last minute grooming on the animals. Today, the official events consisted only of the 4-H dog show and the preliminary round of equine judging.

"Exactly?" Amber filled the word with doubt.

"Yes." Beth nodded. "The rules require a one-minute sit and three-minute down. I've been timing our group for a couple of weeks now."

"Group eight, please enter the ring." A stray sound from the microphone key ended the announcement.

"Wish me luck?"

"Nail it." Beth gave girl and dog a thumbs-up and a smile.

A horse whinnied off to her right. Exhibitors for the afternoon event were unloading contestants from trailers into a temporary corral. From an earlier inspection, Beth was aware the corral structure consisted of metal gates attached to each other with steel fence posts at intervals for sturdiness.

A thread of anxiety ascended Beth's neck. She ignored the dog judging ring long enough to count the tweens and dogs around the ice chest again. All present and on good behavior. Even the beagle had given up his excavation attempt and was resting his head on his owner's foot.

Adjusting her white ball cap with the green 4-H logo, Beth settled her attention on Amber and Tango as they took their positions in the group of five handlers and dogs. She forced her gaze away from the judge walking a wide circle.

Leave it. The warning phrase, practiced for three years now when near attractive men, came and went in an instant. The judge drew her attention like forbidden food tempted her dogs, so instead, she methodically moved her gaze to the several dozen spectators on the lower portion of the grandstand. They were a mix of supportive parents, dog show enthusiasts, and the curious.

"Sit your dogs." The judge faced the participants and paused until all the animals were in position. "Leave your dogs."

Beth held her breath as Amber walked away from Tango, turned, and stood stiff.

Tango lifted her nose as if catching an interesting scent, but she didn't move her body from the required pose.

"Return to your dogs." The judge walked in a slow circle while jotting notes on the clipboard. When he stopped, he was on Beth's side of the ring, less than six feet away.

Beth rubbed at another nervous shiver down her neck as two horses started a verbal quarrel in their new quarters. Pay attention. She took a few seconds to check on the other children, who were still obeying directions.

"Down your dogs." The command was quickly followed by the next. "Leave your dogs."

Attention back on the judging ring, Beth sighed with relief when Tango remained still in the Sphinx-like position as Amber walked away. If the shepherd messed up, it would be either at the moment of separation or in the final fifteen seconds. Beth could sympathize with the latter. Three minutes without moving was difficult for humans too, even adults like her.

As the judge walked in slow, confident steps around the handlers to the far side of the ring, Beth's gaze moved with him. No ring. Blue eyes and almost invisible brows.

Unbidden, she recited under her breath portions of his bio from the official program. "Jackson Dray. Active in North Wisconsin Working Dogs Association. Formerly judged 4-H events in Brown County."

She forced her attention away and checked once more on the other club members. Two handlers from other clubs had joined them. She counted four tweens in Lucky Leaf shirts and accounted for the matching dogs before turning back to the judging ring.

"Return to your dogs."

Amber released clenched hands during the return walk, pivoted when beside Tango, and reached down for the leash.

"Dismissed."

A moment later, Amber and Tango followed another pair out of the ring and headed toward her.

Beth sent a big smile and two thumbs-up to them. "Good job. Both of you."

"It was hard. Harder than practice."

"Let's get some water. You both need it." Beth raised her voice on the last two words to compete with the increasingly noisy horses. She saw several handlers among the small herd, catching halters and speaking to the animals. Beth opened the ice chest to retrieve disposable dog dishes and bottles of water. "Water break. Remember. Dogs first."

The canines tugged on leashes and whined. Shouts and whinnies from the horse corral were punctuated with the metallic clang of trailer gates. With the dogs behaving conflicted between the desire for a drink and exploring the arriving horses, she hurried to hand out the final dish and water bottle. She noted several other groups scattered around the racetrack infield and discarded the brief notion of moving. This was a good location, with a clear line of sight to both the judging ring and the fairgrounds traffic.

The noise multiplied from the corral. One, two, then more dogs barked at the commotion. A resounding thud and loud clatter were followed by more shouts and the rumble of restless hooves.

"Hiya! Get up!"

Beth turned in time to see three horses break out of the temporary pen and head straight toward them. They had riders who appeared to be encouraging the escape rather than bringing their mounts under control.

She spread her arms in an attempt to herd her charges away from the approaching steeds. "Run. Now."

** *

Jackson struggled to keep his attention on the words of the ring steward. The increasing activity from the horses made him nervous. He never trusted equines. After one brief, painful encounter when he was a youngster, he figured the best place for a horse was a mile away from his position.

"Hiya! Get up!"

Jackson sensed rather than actually saw the large animals out of control and approaching. "Down!"

He wrapped his arm around the waist of his assistant and brought her to the ground with him. He shielded her with his body and rested his forehead against the fine sawdust. Please, God, miss us. He held his breath as the first huge shadow leaped over them. An instant later, a second horse jumped clear.

A single police siren added an insistent voice to the confusion of horses, dogs, and humans. A heartbeat later, second and third sirens joined the chorus.

"Not yet," he shouted near the ring steward's ear.

Counting seconds, Jackson was at four when the third horse bumped his legs while passing over them. He rolled to his left, checked for any more attackers, and reached for a leash trailing in the sawdust.

"Clear," the ring steward said, pushing to a sitting position. "Are you hurt?"

"No." Jackson scrambled toward another loose dog.

A moment later, two leashes in one hand, he tested the standing position. It worked better than expected. No doubt he'd have a huge bruise tomorrow, but that was better than his previous encounter with a horse.

He offered a hand to his assistant, flinching when all his weight went on the bruised leg. "Are you still in one piece?"

She brushed sawdust off her arms, surveying the shambles around them. "I think so. Kids, dogs, and horses. What could possibly go wrong?"

Jackson nodded at her smile and good humor.

As the sirens were silenced one by one, the number of barking and howling dogs decreased until a relative calm settled across the area. Jackson's attention was briefly drawn to a knot of spectators gathered on the far side of the racetrack. Kids, dogs, and a generous sprinkling of adults were gathered around the deputies as the three riders were forced to dismount and loaded into patrol cars. Additional deputies gathered reins and held the restless horses.

Jackson scanned the area and sighed with relief at the sight of adults calming the horses remaining in the corral. He continued sweeping his gaze in a wide circle, paused, and smiled. The woman with the auburn ponytail was speaking to a girl in a white 4-H club shirt.

After a quick visual inspection of his two canine charges, he walked toward her.

"Are these yours?" Jackson held back the shepherd lunging toward the girl.

"Tango." The girl wrapped both arms around the dog's neck and muttered into thick fur.

"Nice reunion."

The woman looked at him with hazel eyes flecked with gold. "Thank you, Mr. Dray."

He swallowed, unable to form a word for an instant. Freckles. He feared she'd hear his heart racing over the continued shouts of handlers calling for their dogs. He'd noticed her the first time she sent a team into the ring this morning, and he'd tried for a closer look without success during the long downs. Drinking in the sight of her now, he memorized a height of five eight or nine, average build, and a mouth quick to smile.

"Crystal Springs?" He pointed at her shirt. The tiny village of 522 was his new address, as of four days ago. "I know the place."

"That makes you part of a small, select group." She smiled before tapping the girl's shoulder. "Amber. Manners."

"Thank you for finding Tango, Mr. Mr.... Judge."

"Mr. Dray. And you're welcome. It's easy to see you're special to each other."

"A good team." The girl took a proper hold on the leash. "That's what Ms. Cosgrove calls us."

He turned his attention back to the leader. "And would you be Ms. Cosgrove?"

"Beth." She offered her hand. "Project leader for Lucky Leaf 4-H Club."

"Jackson." He managed to keep the handshake short and professional by ignoring the hum of energy at the touch of her skin. "Now, do you know the handler for—"

"Rupert." A middle-aged lady holding the hand of a reluctant boy hurried over from their left.

The All-American dog with floppy ears beside Jackson whipped his tail in a show of recognition at the approaching pair.

Jackson squatted and found the tag on the dog's collar. "Rupert. 715-888-5555."

"No more adventures, Rupert." The boy took the leash and accepted sloppy kisses on his hand.

Jackson exchanged a few pleasantries with the new arrivals. Then he directed a smile at Beth. "Excuse me. I've got duties in the ring."

He turned around and walked away without glancing back. If he looked at Beth's face, with that charming butterfly array of freckles, he'd never finish his judging duties. He repeated her name under his breath as he gathered the last of the papers that had scattered when the table was overturned. Places where they would cross paths in the normal business of day-to-day life popped up as he handed the ring steward ribbons to arrange in neat rows on the awards table. Crystal Springs was tiny. It would be surprising not to see her again.

Cosgrove. He turned the name over in his mind a few times but didn't find it familiar. Tonight he'd slip the name into conversation with his brother and sister-in-law. Most of the families had deep roots in the community. While he and his brother, Linc, had been raised in another portion of the state, their family, ending with their grandparents, had lived and farmed in Crystal Springs since the last quarter of the nineteenth century.

"Here." The ring steward pressed a bottle of water into his hand. "Drink up while I check if the speaker system still works."

"Be sure to announce that no one was disqualified today." He cracked the seal on the drink.

"It's on the top of my script."

Three at a time, Jackson presented the white and red ribbons to the pairs of youngsters and dogs. He posed for photographs with each small group. The blue ribbon winners were called individually for their awards. By the time he had two awards left, his face ached from smiles and sunburn.

The PA system stuttered to life. "Reserve champion for River County 4-H Dog Obedience, Novice Class, is Amber Zimmer and Tango. Please give them a nice round of applause."

Jackson presented the ribbon to Amber and risked a glance at the ring entrance. Beth Cosgrove stood straight and proud, the other members of her group beside her, all clapping for the club member.

After presenting the ribbon for champion to a young man with a Norwegian elkhound, Jackson concentrated on packing up the records and equipment. By the time he looked out to the infield, Beth and her group weren't within sight.

"Plans for the afternoon?" the ring steward ventured.

Jackson lifted a box for the fifty-something woman and walked beside her to her van. "What's a good lunch spot in Wagoner? I'm not real familiar with the place." Yet.

On Monday, he'd be starting his new job as an associate at the law firm of White & White. He felt certain that within several weeks, he'd learn the town, or at least the few blocks surrounding the courthouse.

"Wagoner only has one traditional café, smack dab in downtown. Fast food place between here and there. Corner Bar serves a good Reuben. That's on the highway, west of downtown. Near the motel."

"Sounds like a good place to try." He discarded the notion of stopping at the fast food place. It would likely be overwhelmed with leaders giving their dog handlers a treat. A local tavern would suit him fine before he headed back to his brother's orchard on the hill outside of Crystal Springs.

His afternoon plans included getting at least a portion of his office corner organized and taking a good look at the antique cash register. As the brother with the better mechanical aptitude, he'd been assigned to fix the business machine. He tried to recall particulars of the cash register and failed. The other evening, Mona, his sister-in-law, had unveiled it while he moved the last of a lumber pile out of the designated orchard sales area. The plan was to use it when they opened to the public for retail sales at the end of the month.

Division of labor at the orchard was falling into a familiar pattern. Linc either handled or supervised all things to do with the apple trees. Mona showed a natural talent for marketing, and they all contributed to the business end by keeping accurate records.

A few minutes later, Jackson waited for traffic at the mouth of the parking lot. A silver van eased past, driven by a woman with an auburn ponytail. Lucky Leaf. My lucky day.

Acknowledgments:

Many people have contributed to this story. I'd like to especially recognize the members of Missouri Romance Writers of America for their continuing education and support.
Craig Schultz contributed generous time and expertise concerning apple orchards.
And to Lois Scorgie for support and thoughtful questions that strengthened the story from beginning to end.

About the author:

Raised in a household filled with books, it was only natural that Ellen Parker grew into an avid reader. She turned to writing as a second career and enjoys spinning the type of story which appeals to multiple generations. She encourages her readers to share her work with mother or daughter – or both.
Ellen currently lives in St. Louis. When not guiding characters to "happily ever after" she's apt to be reading, walking in the neighborhood, or tending her tiny garden. You can find her on the web at www.ellenparkerwrites.wordpress.com and www.facebook.com/ellenparkerwrites.

Made in the USA
Columbia, SC
22 January 2023